ONE PITCH
AT A TIME

Also by C.W. Spooner

Street Cred
Like a Flower in the Field
Yeah, What Else?
Children of Vallejo
'68 – A Novel

ONE PITCH AT A TIME

a novella

C.W. SPOONER

ONE PITCH AT A TIME
A NOVELLA

iUniverse books may be ordered through booksellers or by contacting:

iUniverse
1663 Liberty Drive
Bloomington, IN 47403
www.iuniverse.com
844-349-9409

ISBN: 978-1-6632-1157-6 (sc)
ISBN: 978-1-6632-1156-9 (e)

Library of Congress Control Number: 2020920615

Print information available on the last page.

iUniverse rev. date: 04/20/2021

For Vallejo High School alumni everywhere
"Apaches Forever"

GOLD RIDGE

Gold Ridge in the Sierra foothills of California bills itself "The Gem of the Mother Lode," and driving through on Highway 49, one can see why. The town came into existence in the early 1850s when gold-bearing quartz deposits were discovered deep beneath the earth. Historic buildings clustered in the downtown district are survivors of that time, restored, remodeled, and shored-up many times through the years. Old neighborhoods are proud of the stately Victorian homes, many of them passed down through generations of the Cornish miners who came from the United Kingdom to work in the hard-rock mines.

When the mines played out, the city declined, and merchants in the downtown area boarded their windows, locked the doors, and walked away. But like many towns in the Mother Lode, Gold Ridge was just waiting to be rediscovered.

Today, it is a destination, a quaint hamlet of eighteen thousand souls that attracts visitors seeking a respite from the crowded cities in the Central Valley and the Bay Area. They come for the funky Gold Rush vibe, the array of upscale restaurants, the galleries that support a thriving art community, and an acclaimed theater company that presents a half-dozen plays each year.

Aside from tourism, the city centers around its schools, especially Gold Ridge Union High, where every student activity, from marching band to football to the debate team, is supported with enthusiasm. And there is a welcome upstart: Gold Ridge Community College, boasting a student body nearing four thousand, offering a two-year degree and a path to the University of California and State University systems.

The Gem of the Mother Lode, indeed. But Gold Ridge is also a community of real people. The majority are Caucasian, with a smattering of Hispanic, Asian, and African American. Some are successful and enjoy the fruits of their considerable accomplishments, while others struggle to get by; most are caught somewhere in between.

These good people have tales to tell about life in a perilous time. The question is, how best to tell their stories? Like the men from Cornwall, we can take pickaxe and shovel in hand and begin chipping away. Better yet, a keyboard and a blank screen.

1

There is an icon in the town of Gold Ridge and his name is Robert Quinn Crutchfeld, known affectionately as Crusty Bob. A vigorous octogenarian, he was the owner/editor of *The Beacon*, a weekly newspaper published every Friday for forty years, a tabloid chock full of national and local news, sports and movie listings, not to mention Mr. Crutchfeld's weekly column. He called his feisty missive "The Corner of First and Main," in honor of the historic building that housed *The Beacon*. The townsfolk simply referred to both—the building and the column—as "Crusty's Corner."

The print edition died shortly after New Year's Day, 2005, a casualty of shrinking ad revenue. The loss hit the community hard. But Bob Crutchfeld was not finished. He launched a website and continued to post his column, much to the delight of his enthusiastic subscribers. He even adopted the popular nickname, just to show his appreciation.

And so, with many stories to tell, we begin with Mr. Crutchfeld.

October 26, 2018
Crusty's Corner
Halloween is upon us and to make things even scarier, mid-term elections are just around the

corner. With Democrats and Republicans screaming past each other and Congress mired in gridlock, we decided to take a break and visit one of our favorite people on the sparkling campus of Gold Ridge Community College.

Harlon Millburn, the revered skipper of the GRCC baseball team, is busy these days directing fall practice. Thirty-five young men, give or take, turn out each afternoon to showcase their talents, hoping to win a coveted uniform for the 2019 season. The competition is fierce, given the fact that Coach Millburn must cut his squad to twenty-five by the time winter break rolls around. I asked the venerable leader for his assessment of fall ball so far. He responded with his usual candor.

"You know, Bob, it all begins out there on the bump. You must have pitching to compete in our league, and I think we have a pretty good crop this year. They've been looking strong in intra-squad games, but the real test will come when we scrimmage against our conference rivals."

I asked about the outlook for offense and defense, and the skipper was ready with his answer.

"Our lineup should be strong, at least through the five-spot in the batting order. And I've seen good leather around the infield and outfield positions. We're a small school, but I think we will be competitive in the Mountain-Valley Conference."

Competitive would be nice—for a change. The Eagles have yet to post a winning record through their seven seasons of existence. That said, I can't wait for mid-January when the 2019 campaign begins. Go Eagles!

—R.Q. Crutchfeld

2

On the campus of Gold Ridge Community College, carved out of the pine forest, a beautiful baseball diamond basked in the October sun. A fall scrimmage was underway, the home team taking on a rival from the Sacramento Valley. Fall baseball was all about development and preparation for the regular season which runs from mid-January through Memorial Day. The winnowing process, cutting the team to twenty-five players, was tough—sometimes brutal.

In the seventh inning, a new pitcher entered the game for the Gold Ridge Eagles. He was tall, a shade under six four, broad of shoulder and narrow of waist, and carried himself with supreme confidence, like a man among boys. He walked the first batter on six pitches. The next hitter clubbed a towering drive that cleared the center field fence for a two-run homerun. Another walk was followed by a line drive that clanged off the chain-link fence in right field, the runner scoring from first, the hitter sliding safely into third.

Head coach Harlon Millburn took a step from the dugout. Was it time to stop the bleeding, bring in another pitcher? No, not yet. He decided to let the young man weather the storm. A long fly ball backed the left fielder up against the fence to make the catch as the runner tagged and scored from third. The next batter lined a ball into the right field corner for a double and Coach had seen enough. With one out, four runs had scored, and every batted ball had been scorched. Millburn walked to the mound, took the ball from the pitcher, and signaled to the bullpen for relief.

The tall, strong, formerly confident pitcher walked to the dugout, his eyes fixed on the grass. It was a pattern, a trend throughout the fall practice season. Every chance to take the mound and show his talent and experience had ended in failure. But the fire in his belly could not accept defeat. He stuffed his gear into an equipment bag and stormed out of the dugout, heading for the locker room where the team trainer would wrap his right arm in bags of ice.

The scrimmage ended with the setting sun and Coach Millburn made his way to his office adjacent to the locker room. He sent one of his assistants to summon the battered pitcher for a frank discussion. The coach hated doing it, but it must be done. The young man, Brett Corcoran, entered his office.

"Sit down, Brett." He motioned to a chair in front of his desk. "We need to talk."

Brett took a seat. He didn't speak.

Millburn continued. "Son, this just isn't working out, certainly not the way we hoped."

"Look, Coach, I know I've had some bad outings—"

"Bad isn't the word for it, Brett. Let's face it, it's been a disaster. I think it's time to call a spade a spade."

"But Coach—"

"I'm sorry, son. You're welcome to stick around until winter break, but when we come back for the regular season, I won't have a uniform for you."

"Coach, you know what I can do. You know what I did in high school. I dominated! I had scouts at every game. I was a prospect—"

"Yeah, I know all that. You were a stud, "Bullet Brett" Corcoran, a sure thing, one of the best to play in this town. And then you left the game, enlisted in the Army right after graduation, though I could never figure out why. I know you were in Iraq. Two tours, right? I'm sure you saw stuff a guy your age shouldn't have to see. I honor your service, I really do." The older man stopped for a deep breath. "Here's the bottom line, Brett. You are a thrower, not a pitcher. I need pitchers. You're not a prospect anymore. You're a project, and I don't have the time or the resources to take on a project. Sorry, son, but that's my decision."

Coach Millburn stood to offer his hand. The meeting was over. The young man hesitated, then rose slowly to take the gnarled old grip. He left the office, cleaned out his locker, and walked away, his cap pulled low to hide the tears.

3

It was a short trip to the Veterans Affairs clinic in Auburn, no more than twenty minutes on a good day. The modern building was situated on the corner of Highway 49 and Bell Road, surrounded by an upscale collection of shops and restaurants. Brett Corcoran had a standing appointment with a VA counselor every Wednesday afternoon. He showed up for most of the appointments, though he called and cancelled a few, if he could think of an excuse—any excuse. He didn't relish talking about his "issues."

Brett pulled into the parking lot with minutes to spare. He made his way into the building to the tiny waiting room and announced himself to the receptionist.

"Have a seat, Mr. Corcoran. The doctor will be with you soon." The girl behind the counter flashed a compassionate smile.

He tried to return the smile. *I'll bet she sees a dish full of assorted nuts.* Brett took a seat and picked up a copy of *Sports Illustrated.* The date on the cover told him it was more than a year old. He tossed it back on the small end table just as the door to the inner office opened.

"Brett! Good to see you. Come on in." Doctor Michael Bowman extended his hand and Brett shook it firmly.

The doctor stood about five nine with his shoes on. He wore wrinkled khaki pants and a golf shirt with an alligator logo. A small paunch extended over his belt. His short brown hair was styled and neatly trimmed. Brett judged him to be in his early forties. He followed Bowman down a short hall and into a compact office. An oak desk and high-backed leather chair took up most of the space. Diplomas lined the wall behind the desk. Brett took one of the chairs that faced the doctor.

"So, Brett, it's been a while. I take it you've been busy." He opened a file folder on his desk and scanned his notes. "Tell me... how are you doing?"

Here we go. I tell him I'm fine and he knows I'm lying. "Yeah... well...better, I think. I mean I've felt better lately. By the way, sorry I had to cancel our last couple of appointments. Had to work. You know how that goes."

"You've got a job? That's great! And you're still enrolled at the community college up there?"

"Yeah, I'm working at a sporting goods store. But I dropped out of school."

"Oh? Why is that?" Dr. Bowman's brow narrowed.

Does he really give a shit? I doubt it. "Ah...it's a long story, Dr. Bowman."

"Hey, we've got plenty of time, Brett. Tell me about it."

Brett provided a recap of his failed attempt to make the Gold Ridge Community College baseball team, the struggles he'd faced in fall practice, and his final meeting with Coach Millburn.

"That really sucks, Brett. But why drop out of school?" The doctor scribbled notes on a steno pad.

Yeah, well fuck you too, Bowman. Why do anything? Why don't I become a VA counselor so I can give half-assed advice to guys with PTSD? "It's just...I don't know, it pissed me off, okay? Millburn pissed me off! I mean that's why I was there, to play baseball. I'm no scholar. I'm not looking to earn a Ph.D. or some shit like that..." Brett raised his voice in tandem with the heat rising on his neck.

Anger. That's what it was all about. Why was he so angry nearly all the time? Why was he on the verge of exploding at the slightest provocation? They both knew why.

Brett was angry when he joined the Army, desperate to get out of Gold Ridge and away from his father. And two tours in Iraq had sealed the deal. He'd challenge anyone to serve in that endless war—a war with no path to victory, with nothing but bad outcomes—and not come away angry. Blood and money poured into the desert and nothing to show for it. Brainless leadership and no way out.

Brett sparred with Dr. Bowman for fifty minutes, never landing a clean blow, absorbing shots to the head and the gut. Was it all for nothing?

"Our time's up, Brett. By the way, how are you sleeping?"

"Not bad. Okay. Some bad nights. You know—"

"Are you taking the medication I prescribed?"

"Yeah. I mean, sometimes. It helps me sleep, but I wake up feeling dopey, you know?"

"That's a common side effect. Take it earlier in the evening. That should help it clear your system. See you next week?"

"Yeah, sure." *I can't freakin' wait, asshole!*

He came in angry. He left wanting to punch Bowman in the face. Brett sat in his car in the parking lot for a long time before he started the engine.

4

The crowd at Denny's was lively and loud at 2:00 a.m., filling most of the booths that ran the length of the plate glass windows. It was a popular place on the weekend, open all night, ready to serve workers coming off the late shift, plus the usual corps of drunks with the munchies. One such group gathered near the cash register, saying their goodbyes after an evening celebrating the close of a business deal. They were dressed in rumpled business suits, ties loosened, shirt collars unbuttoned, all four of them likely beyond the threshold that would qualify for DUI, and yet all four would drive home on the narrow mountain roads. The tall one, Donald T. Corcoran, in his early fifties with neatly trimmed brown hair graying at the temples, insisted on picking up the tab. After all, the other three reported to him, called him boss, or chief, or dipshit if he wasn't there to hear it.

Don shooed them out the door and made his way to the register, reaching for his wallet. He handed the check and his company credit card to the hostess who asked politely if everything was satisfactory. Before Don could answer, he looked to his right, to the short counter with a half-dozen stools. There he saw an old black man wearing a tattered jacket and faded jeans, his salt and pepper hair revealing a bald spot the size of a bagel. The man's head nodded, dipping lower

11

and lower toward a plate of eggs-over-easy. Don's eyes widened. He knew this man. He finished his transaction with the hostess and walked to the counter, just as the man's nose hit the eggs.

"Webb? Hey, Webb. Wake up, Coach." Don shook the man's shoulder, then again, until he slowly straightened and opened his eyes. "Coach Webb Johnson, is that really you?"

Johnson blinked his eyes, reached for a napkin and wiped his nose. "Well, I'll be damned. You're Don...what the hell was the last name? Corcoran! Am I right? Don Corcoran."

"That's right. God, Coach, it's been a long, long time. How the hell are you?"

The old man chuckled. "I'll give you three guesses, and the first two don't count." He fumbled in his jacket and the back pocket of his jeans. "Where's my damn wallet?"

"Don't worry about it, Coach. Let me get your breakfast."

Don picked up the check from the counter. Johnson pivoted on the stool and attempted to stand. A moment later he was flat on his back, his feet in the air.

"Whoa! You okay, Coach? Here, give me your hand." Don braced himself and helped the old man to his feet. "There you go, Webb. Where are you staying?"

"Got a room, south side of town."

"I'll give you a ride home. Do you have a car here?'

"Yeah."

"No problem. We'll collect your vehicle tomorrow. You're not driving anymore tonight."

Don paid the hostess. He clamped his arm firmly around Webb's slim body, one arm slung over his shoulder. They exited the restaurant and headed for the parking lot, one shaky step at a time.

The Bitter Creek Hotel was built in the late forties during the boom that followed World War II. It was a three-story palace with a marble-floored lobby that was a bit over the top for its time. Its time passed long ago. Situated on the southern edge of town, it was a landmark in a neighborhood that had fallen on hard times. The old hotel had been converted to residence units, each sporting a kitchenette and a full bath. Maintenance had been deferred since the Carter administration, but the residents didn't complain. The price was right.

A silver BMW pulled into the parking lot on the south side of the building and two men emerged, one white, one black. They entered the hotel and climbed the stairs to the second floor. Webb Johnson called unit 201 home. He unlocked the door and hit the light switch.

"Thanks for gettin' me home, Don. Damn, I can't believe it, after all these years, Don Corcoran bringin' me home."

"No problem, Webb. I'll come by tomorrow morning and we'll go retrieve your car. How 'bout 10:30, maybe 11:00?"

"Make it 11:00. I need my beauty rest."

"How long you been here, Coach?"

"Don't call me Coach. I've been back about six months. Hard to believe, but I missed the old town."

"Hard to believe? Why is that?" Don knew the answer. He wanted the conversation to continue.

"Come on, man. You know the story. Couple of DUIs, couple of drunk and disorderlies, and the school district was going to fire my ass. But I foxed 'em. I had the age and years of service for my pension. With that and Social Security, I live like a king, as you can plainly see."

"Ever think about coaching again, Webb? You were the best pitching coach I ever had, a great teacher."

"Nah. I put all that shit behind me. Baseball's a young man's game. No place for a burned out old drunk." Webb sat down hard on his bed and began to remove his shoes.

Don looked around the room. The furnishings were meager—a dresser and a small drop-leaf table with two wooden chairs. A door to one side revealed a closet to the left and the bathroom on the right. The kitchenette was neat and clean, a coffee maker and toaster the only small appliances visible. The room needed a fresh coat of paint, but other than that, not bad.

"Okay, Webb. I'll see you in the morning. Get some rest."

The old man had removed his pants, climbed into bed, and pulled the covers up to his chin. He did not answer.

5

The large two-story home was tucked into a clearing in the northern quarter of the four-acre property, surrounded by tall pines and thick underbrush. The access road was wide enough for a single vehicle, requiring one to pull over if a car came from the opposite direction. The circular drive in front of the house was covered in gravel, providing an audible crunch when visitors arrived.

In the sparkling modern kitchen, Don Corcoran filled his favorite mug with coffee, then added a shot of brandy, a little hair of the dog to jumpstart his day. It was just past 10:00 a.m. on Saturday morning and he had promised to meet Webb Johnson by 11:00. Don took a large gulp of coffee, then another. He heard tires crunch on the gravel outside and peered through the window. It was his son, Brett. The front door slammed and a moment later, Brett entered the kitchen.

"Morning, son. Just getting in?"

Brett grunted a greeting and dropped his keys on the counter.

Don knew better than to poke the bear, but he was curious. "Where you been?"

"At Ramona's. Why?" Brett poured a cup of coffee, minus the brandy.

"Getting pretty serious, eh?"

Brett glared at his father. "Is that a problem?"

"No. Just saying, that's all. Am I ever going to meet this girl?"

"Yeah, I suppose. Why the sudden interest?"

Don let the hostility slide. His head was pounding and he didn't need a fight to start the day. He gulped his coffee. "Hey, I ran into someone last night, a real blast from the past."

Brett sipped his coffee and didn't respond.

"Did I ever mention Webster Johnson? Everybody calls him Webb. He was my pitching coach in high school. Great coach, great teacher."

Brett looked up. "Is that the Webb Johnson who played pro ball? For the…"

"The Giants. He was in their organization for a half-dozen years. He's back in town, living at the Bitter Creek."

"Yeah?" Brett looked at his father. "So…is there a point to this story?"

"I don't know, I'm just thinking. Maybe I could get him to work with you. He was a great teacher, the best I ever had, that's for sure."

"Webb Johnson. What is he, in his eighties now?"

"Nah, more like late seventies."

"Oh, swell, Dad. You think this old fart living in a flophouse can fix everything, 'cause back in the day he was hot shit?"

"Look, Brett, I'm just saying he was a hell of a coach. Maybe he can help you. Coach Millburn just cut you loose, you dropped out of school, you're working at the Big 5 for minimum wage. You're twenty-two years old, son. What do you have to lose?"

Brett stared at his father as the silence lengthened. "What makes you think he'd agree to work with me?"

"Hey, all I can do is ask." Don smiled and finished his coffee, convinced the brandy was beginning to help.

Horsetail white clouds floated in from the west, backed by towering gray cumulus. The forecast was for afternoon rain, enough to soak the forest and beat down the fire danger. It had been a dry year and rain was welcome.

Don parked next to the old hotel and trotted up the steps to unit 201. He knocked several times, waiting for an answer. Webb Johnson opened the door.

"Hey, right on time. It really is you. Thought maybe I was havin' a dream. Let me get my jacket." The old man shuffled toward a closet.

Don watched him closely, glad to see a steady gait. "How are you feeling this morning, Webb?"

"Like hammered shit. How you feelin'?"

Don laughed. "Pretty much the same. Come on, let's go get your car."

The ride to Denny's was punctuated with small talk, discussing changes in the town—new buildings, upgrades, the relentless gentrification. Don had an agenda and he steered the conversation to his purpose.

"Webb, I asked last night if you'd ever thought about coaching again—"

"And I said, 'hell no.'"

"You sure about that?"

"Damn sure!"

"And that's your final answer?"

"Jeezus, Corcoran, spit it out. What's on your mind?"

"I know a young man who could use your help. Big, strong, good work ethic. He can touch mid-nineties on the radar gun."

"So why does he need me?"

Don laughed. "Because he needs to learn how to pitch, and you're the guy who can teach him."

"Who is this young man? Have I heard of him?"

"His name is Brett." Don hesitated, then continued. "Brett Corcoran. He's my son."

17

"Your son? Well hell! Why don't you teach him? You know everything I know. Do it your damn self." Webb shook his head and looked out the window.

"He won't listen to me. We don't get along so well. It's a long story." Don thought about sharing but did not go on.

"Long story, my ass. Fathers and sons. It's the oldest damn story in the book."

Don let it rest. He pulled into the parking lot at Denny's and Webb pointed out his battered pickup truck.

"Look, Webb, don't say no right now. Think about it, okay? I'll pay you for your time, make it worth your while. You could use some extra cash…am I right?"

Webb opened the door and turned to look at Don. "You got that right. A dollar ain't worth fifty cents anymore."

"You can name your price, Coach. Do it your way, at your own pace. I'd have only one rule."

"Oh, look out, here it comes. What's your one rule?"

"No booze. You'd have to dry out for the duration, however long it takes."

Webb laughed out loud. "And there it is, folks. The turd in the punchbowl."

Don reached in his shirt pocket, removed a business card, and offered it to the old man. "Just think about it, Webb. My number is on the card. Call me anytime. Okay?"

Webb took the card. He planted his feet on the pavement and lifted himself out of the car. "Thanks for the ride, Corcoran. Now get the hell out of here."

6

January 29, 2019
Crusty's Corner
Growing up in Northern California in the 40s and 50s, I learned certain things at my father's knee. First, San Francisco should be called The City, as if there were only one. Second, Los Angeles was a cultural wasteland, bathed in smog and little else. We were passionate fans of the San Francisco 49ers and equally passionate against the L.A. Rams. As time went on, our loyalties extended to the baseball Giants and basketball Warriors, and we grew to despise the Dodgers and the Lakers.

John Brodie, the old 49er quarterback, spoke for all of us when he said, "We'd look across the line of scrimmage and see those ridiculous helmets with the curling ram horns and it just flat pissed us off."

The 49ers would play the Rams three times each year—once in preseason and twice during league play. A winning year for San Francisco meant taking at least two out of three from the Rams. The rest of the season would take care of itself.

So, here we are in January 2019, and the Rams have found their way back to the L.A. Coliseum, having wandered off to St. Louis for a number of years. Now they are going to meet the New England Patriots in the Super Bowl on February 3.

The burning question for this newsboy is: How can I possibly root for the Los Angeles Rams? I suppose I should make the effort. After all, the Patriots have had an impressive run, racking up five Super Bowl titles under the leadership of coach Bill Belichick and quarterback Tom Brady. It's time for the Pats to move on; their legacy is secure.

But still, it is hard to look at the Rams in their ridiculous helmets and not want to shout, as Viking's quarterback Joe Kapp once did, "F--- you, Rams!"

I'll try to adjust my attitude before kickoff on February 3.

—R.Q. Crutchfeld

7

The Uptown Gallery occupied the first floor of a fine old Victorian. The second floor had been remodeled into a large open space where art classes met. A dozen student-artists sat at their easels sketching a nude model, a young woman seated on a raised platform draped in black material. An instructor wandered among the easels, commenting, coaching, encouraging her students. Tall windows lined the west side of the room, admitting afternoon sunlight that fell across the model's body. The instructor called for a break, directed the class to turn to a fresh page, and asked the young model to strike a different pose. The sketching resumed.

Brett entered the ground floor gallery, waved to the employees working there, and proceeded up the stairs to the studio. He stood at the rear of the room and nodded to the instructor, who smiled in return. Brett scanned the drawings in progress, noted that several were quite good, capturing the light and shadow, not to mention the beauty of the model. And a beauty she was. Her hair long and black, her skin a dark olive tone, her features exquisite—dark eyes, sensuous lips, celestial nose, high cheekbones. There was only one word that applied: stunning.

A grandfather clock in the corner struck the hour and the instructor told the students to stop for the day. She thanked the model and the class gave the young woman a round of applause. The girl lifted a white terrycloth robe from the platform, put it on and tied it at the waist. She stepped down from the platform, slipped on a pair of flipflops, and walked across the floor to where Brett was standing. She stood on tiptoes to kiss his lips.

"Hi, sweetie. How was your day?"

"Good, Ramona. How 'bout you? Looks like a talented class here." Brett scanned the room as the students put away their supplies and stored their work in large portfolios.

"You think so? I never really get to see their work." She glanced over her shoulder.

"I noticed something, call it a random observation." Brett grinned.

"Yeah?"

"Yeah. The female students do a great job capturing your face, all the lovely features."

Ramona laughed. "And the male students?"

"They tend to focus on your body. Especially those beautiful—"

"Oh, stop it!" She laughed and punched his arm. "I'm gonna get dressed. Just sit tight and I'll be right back. Okay?"

"I'll be here." He smiled as she hurried away.

Ramona Hernandez was a formidable young woman, a true force of nature. She was a first-year nursing student in the highly respected program at the community college, and she supported herself waiting tables in upscale restaurants around town while earning extra money as a model. She and Brett Corcoran met on campus and the attraction was immediate and mutual. Their friends thought of them as The Odd Couple—the blonde, blue-eyed jock, and the dark, beautiful, and very serious nursing student.

She emerged from the dressing area, behind a screen at the back of the room, wearing black slacks, a white cotton blouse with a high collar, and low-heeled black pumps. Brett couldn't suppress a smile. No matter what she wore, it looked terrific.

"So…" She looked at him wide-eyed, curious. "We're meeting your dad for dinner?"

"Yeah. Him and his lady friend."

"You say 'lady friend' like it's a disease."

"Yeah, well, there's a lot of history."

"Okay, I'm listening."

Brett felt cornered. He'd put this off as long as possible and now it was too late to keep dodging. They left the old Victorian and walked along the sidewalk heading east. "Ah…remember I told you my mom passed away four years ago."

"Yes."

"It was because of a car accident. My parents' SUV slid off an icy road, slammed into a tree, crushed the passenger side. That's where my mom was sitting. She suffered massive brain trauma, which led to surgery, which led to infection, more surgery, more complications. It took about eight months…but she died. She spent the last month in hospice."

Ramona squeezed his hand and snuggled close. "I'm so sorry, Brett." She paused. "Was alcohol involved in the accident?"

"No. My dad wasn't a drinker—then. It was just wrong place, wrong time. Anyway, my dad's lady friend, Lilly, was Mom's hospice nurse."

"Oh…"

"I walked in on them one night, about a week before Mom died."

"You mean…"

"Yeah, saw them in the act." Brett swallowed hard. "I've tried to understand, Ramona. I really have. But I can't let it go. I can't forgive him. As soon as I graduated high school, I enlisted in the Army and got the hell out of here. You know the rest."

"Oh my God! I don't know what to say. How awful for you. But now you're back, and they're still together?"

"Yeah, off and on. I think she was living at the house until I came home and moved back in. I know she's not an evil person, I mean, she's a nurse for God's sake. It's just…I still can't look her in the eye without wanting to scream."

Ramona was quiet, absorbing the story.

"Oh well," she said. "This should be an interesting evening."

8

Ristorante Ricci was tucked into the corner of an old building that
dated from the 1890s. The original red brick had been exposed on
the interior walls, the tables set with immaculate white tablecloths
and polished silverware, the atmosphere warm and inviting. The
current proprietors were the scions of a large Italian family and their
interpretation of Northern Italian cuisine was praised by food critics
throughout the region. The aroma of garlic sautéed in butter and
olive oil greeted patrons as they entered the friendly surroundings.
A hostess led Ramona and Brett to a table for four and a busboy
appeared quickly with water and a basket of warm, crusty bread.

Brett checked his phone. "Dad texted they'll be a few minutes
late."

"Okay. I'm going to make a quick trip to the lady's room. I'll
be right back."

Brett relaxed amid the buzz of the busy restaurant. He dipped a
piece of bread in olive oil and took a bite. He saw his father hold the
front door open for his date as they entered. Brett waved and they
made their way to the table. He braced himself, determined to make
this evening drama free. Polite greetings were exchanged and they

took their seats. Brett had to admit, Lilly was an attractive woman, tall and slim with auburn hair cut short and neatly styled.

Don looked around. "Man, I could really use a martini. They make a great one here. Where's our waiter?"

"Make it two." Lilly smiled. "Is Ramona joining us, Brett?"

"Yeah, she'll be right here."

Don looked up, beyond Brett's left shoulder. "Ah, here comes our waitress." He raised his hand to flag her down. "Miss, can we get two very dry Beefeater martinis, with a couple of olives each? How 'bout you, son?"

Brett turned to see Ramona standing by the table. He stood and held her chair as she moved gracefully to sit down. "She's not the waitress, Dad. This is Ramona. Ramona, my father Don and his friend Lilly."

"Hello. It's nice to meet you." Ramona extended her hand to Lilly and then Don.

Don tried to laugh. "Oh my God! I saw you coming and I just assumed—" He flinched as Lilly kicked him under the table.

Ramona smiled. "It's okay. I get that a lot. But usually in Mexican restaurants." She burst out laughing, a deep belly-laugh that Brett loved. In a moment, they were laughing with her, the awkward situation disarmed.

The evening had nowhere to go but up. Ramona and Lilly quickly found common ground with a discussion of nursing school and hospice practice. Brett and Don focused on sports in general, the upcoming Super Bowl in particular.

"So, whataya think, Rams or Patriots?" Don smiled across the table.

"Ah, I don't have a dog in that fight. Just hope it's a good game."

"Let's watch it together. We'll bring in some munchies. What do you like, wings or pizza?"

Brett hesitated. It had been many years since he'd watched the Super Bowl with his dad. His father was reaching out, offering a path forward. "Sure. That'll be…good. I love Buffalo wings. Can we bring anything?"

After a rocky beginning, the evening was saved.

Brett and Ramona cuddled, spoon fashion, a blanket pulled up against the January chill. Ramona shared a two-bedroom apartment with a girl who was seldom there, having found a potential soulmate with a place of his own. Ramona's bedroom held the bare necessities—an overstuffed chair, a dresser, and a double bed with a firm mattress. The windows faced south with a view of the college campus, and on this night, the light of a new moon spilled through the blinds.

"Brett, are you awake, sweetie?"

Brett pulled her closer. "Yeah, I'm awake."

"Can we talk about tonight?"

His heart was full. In that moment, she could ask for anything. "Sure. What about?"

"Your dad seems to drink a lot."

"I know. Worries me a little. That's new, since Mom died."

"Think you should talk to him?"

"Yeah…probably."

She was quiet for a moment. "Lilly seems nice. Is it okay if I say that?"

"You two really hit it off."

"She's committed to nursing, very kind and caring. I'm gonna be a nurse, but I don't know if I could do what she does in hospice."

Brett hesitated, but he had to admit it. "She was great with my mom."

"Listen…remember when we first met? On campus at the student union?"

"Yeah. I remember you were wearing those jeans I like." Brett smiled.

"I knew right then that we would be together. I was in a relationship, with a guy who's a junior at Cal, but I started to break it off, just like that. And then you finally asked me out. Remember?"

"Yep. We went out for pizza and beer."

"And talked for hours, and then came back here to my bed. The next morning, I was embarrassed and a little shocked, because that's not me. It's not who I am. I've never been casual or easy about sex. How do you explain attraction like that? Who can explain chemistry?" She paused. "I'm not saying that's what your dad and Lilly have between them, but if it is, I understand. It doesn't excuse what they did. But maybe it explains it."

"Uh...okay—" Brett wasn't sure what to say.

"You said tonight you were trying to understand, trying to forgive. Right?"

"Yes."

"All I'm saying is, keep trying. He's your father. She's a good person. Just keep trying."

Ramona was quiet then. Brett tightened his arms around her and kissed the back of her head, sure of one thing: many people give you advice; very few give you wisdom.

9

The battered pickup wound its way down the narrow road and onto the gravel driveway. The driver, an old black man, stepped out of the truck and looked around, impressed by the well-maintained home and the surrounding property. In his eyes it was a castle in the pines. Don Corcoran's business card read, "Vice President – Marketing / The Sherman Group," obviously a damn good gig. The front door opened and Don stepped out onto the porch.

"Webb! You're here. Any trouble finding the place?"

"Nah, no problem. My phone's got the GPS gizmo. Nice place you got here, Don. Or should I call you Mr. Vice President?"

"Just plain Don will be fine," he laughed. "I'm really glad you called, Webb."

"Let's be straight. I'm not committing just yet. You said you had some video for me to watch. I'll take a look and see if I can do any good for your boy. Got it?"

"Agreed. Come on in, let me show you what I have."

Don led the way through a brief tour of the lower floor, then down a flight of stairs to a basement rec room that featured a pool table, a leather couch, and a large flatscreen TV. A video camera was tethered to the TV by a long thin cable. Don demonstrated play, stop, rewind, all the functions. "I've got Brett's last four outings recorded, a total of seven innings, all shot from behind home plate. You'll hear a voice calling out velocity readings. Two members of the pitching staff are there, one charting pitches, the other manning the radar gun."

"Okay. Let's take a look." Webb made himself comfortable on the couch and manipulated the buttons. The screen lit up with the image of a young man on the pitcher's mound, winding up and delivering a pitch. Webb looked at Don. "Are you going to hang around and bug me while I do this? Why don't you go take a hike?"

"Oh…okay." Don stood and headed for the stairs. "Need some water, Webb? Maybe a cold beer?"

"No thanks. Haven't had a drink for about a month, by the way."

He didn't add that he'd also found a local AA meeting to attend. It wasn't Webb's first time on the merry-go-round.

"Good for you, Coach!"

"Don't call me Coach. Yet. Now leave me be."

Webb hit the stop button one last time and turned to find Don standing at the foot of the stairs. He motioned him over and Don took a seat opposite the old coach. Webb began slowly.

"Okay, here's what I see. You could call this the 'seven innings from hell.' Young Brett got tattooed, blasted, balls ripped all over the lot. So, you were right, he needs to learn how to pitch. Here's the good news. He has nice mechanics, which is important. If that's what you taught him, then good job, Dad."

Don smiled but kept quiet.

"Another good thing. The kid throws hard. Most of his fastballs were low-nineties, and looking at his build, I think there's more in the tank."

"I agree." Don waited. "Go ahead, Webb."

"So, why is he gettin' hit so hard? Pretty simple. He's out there throwin', just trying to blow the ball by the hitters. I'm sure it worked in high school, but it ain't gonna work at the college level where guys can hit. He has little command, falls behind in the count, then has to groove a pitch to avoid ball four. His curve ball is terrible. I never saw one close to the strike zone. And he apparently has no changeup. So, he's out there with a wild-ass fastball, one that has little movement, by the way. The result is he's gettin' his ass kicked." He paused. "And that's the name of that tune."

"Can you help him, Webb?"

"Look, Don, you got to understand something right up front. My ways are 'old school.' I'm a dinosaur. Nobody buys what I'm sellin' anymore. Now it's all this Big Data, high-tech shit—Statcast, TrackMan, PITCHfx, Rapsoto. It's all about spin rates and spin efficiency, and cameras that catch the exact release from the fingertips. They talk about 'pitch design.' I don't do pitch design, Don. Why should a smart young guy listen to me?"

Don didn't hesitate. "Because all that high-tech shit won't do any good if he hasn't learned what you teach. I really believe that, Webb."

Webb stared at the floor for a long time, weighing the pros and cons, the dollars and sense of it. Finally, he looked at Don. "Okay, if we can agree on the money angle, I'll give it my best shot."

Don jumped off the couch, his arms open wide. Was he looking for a hug? Webb made sure it didn't happen, offering his hand instead. They headed up the stairs to find pen and paper to seal the deal.

10

March 11, 2019

Crusty's Corner

The March 4 cover of *Time* magazine made me smile. It depicts President Donald Trump at his desk in the Oval Office, glancing furtively to his right. Behind him, peering through the windowpanes, is the impressive array of Democrats currently running for president.

Septuagenarians are front and center: Joe Biden, Elizabeth Warren, Bernie Sanders. Some younger folks, too: Kamala Harris, Cory Booker, Beto O'Rourke, Stacey Abrams. In the back row, three people with interesting ideas: Amy Klobuchar, Julian Castro, Mayor Pete.

I'll admit there were a few faces that stumped me. *Who the heck is that?* A quick trip to Google cleared it up: Kirsten Gillibrand, Tulsi Gabbard, Sherrod Brown. And to top things off, two billionaires: Mike Bloomberg and Howard Schultz. At least I think that's Howard behind the Starbuck's cup.

If my math is correct, that's fifteen faces out of a field of twenty-four declared candidates—and counting. We're going to need a bigger window.

Thomas Perez, Chair of the Democratic National Committee, has come up with some interesting rules regarding who will qualify for the debates beginning in June. It is a formula based on the number of donors across a number of states, plus 1% in each of three qualifying polls. There may be something about standing on one foot and touching your left ear with your right hand. I can't recall.

One thing is clear: the most important element to bring to the debate stage will be a pair of sharp elbows.

—R.Q. Crutchfeld

11

Ramona turned over in bed and reached for Brett, expecting to find him there, ready to hold her while she drifted back to sleep. He wasn't there. She opened her eyes, turned and reached for her cell phone on the bedside table. It was past 3:00 a.m. She threw back the covers, put her feet on the floor, and waited for her head to clear. She walked out of the bedroom and down the hall to the kitchen. Brett was standing near the window that looked out over the parking lot toward the college campus.

"Hey. Whatcha doin'?" She joined him by the window and he wrapped her in his arms.

"Hard to sleep tonight, babe."

"Just not tired?" She looked up, sleepy-eyed.

"No. I close my eyes and bad scenes happen."

"You mean from Iraq?"

"Yeah. I keep seeing our convoy, the MRAP in front going into the air on a fireball, the blast hitting our vehicle. I can't shut it down. I didn't want to keep you awake, so—"

"You weren't keeping me awake." She hugged his waist. "Tell me again, what's an Em-rap?"

"Mine-resistant Ambush Protected. It's a super-armored personnel carrier."

"Oh, right." She waited, hoping he'd continue. "Are you going to see that VA doctor this week?"

"Yeah. Probably." Brett stared out the window.

"Is he helping you, Brett?"

"Good question. I don't know. He's a nice enough guy. But he's never served in combat, never been in a forward post. I just keep asking myself—how can he know anything? Why should I listen to him?"

"Maybe the important thing is he listens to you?"

Brett looked down at her and smiled. "When did you get so smart?"

She laughed. "How's this for smart? We'll have a glass of milk and I think we have some Oreos left. Come on, babe. Milk and cookies and then we'll get some sleep." She took his hand and led him to the kitchen table.

Ramona liked to break her Oreos apart and lick the icing. Brett was a dunker, partial to soft, saturated goodness. The cold milk was perfect.

"Brett, I have to ask a question. I mean, if you don't want to talk about it, I understand."

"What do you want to know?"

"Okay…when we watch the news and a report about Iraq comes on, I see you tense up, and I can hear the anger in your voice. Is it all because of what happened when your convoy got blown up?"

Brett was quiet. She wondered if he was ready to open up.

"It's the stupidity, Ramona. The utter stupidity of the whole thing. I mean, we get a report of some hostiles out in the area. So, we load up in the MRAPs and convoy down the road to fight the bad guys. And we hit a roadside bomb. Big freakin' surprise! Concussions, broken bones, broken teeth, whatever. But by God, we're gonna keep on driving down those roads. Nobody is gonna stop us. When it started, back in 2003, guys were convoying in unarmed Humvees. Arms and legs blown off, dead soldiers. So, the Army put armor on the Humvees. Still murder and mayhem, more

dead soldiers. Finally, we got the MRAPs, big honkin' muthas, able to withstand any kind of IED. So now, no lost arms and legs, just broken heads. Brains shaken so bad you live with it the rest of your life. But by God, we're gonna keep saddling up in convoys and driving down those goddamn roads."

His voice rose, his hands trembled on the table.

"They say fatalities are down ninety percent since we got the MRAPs, and the brass slap themselves on the back and hand out awards. But what if your buddies are in the ten percent? What if *you* are in the ten percent? Are you any less dead? Ah, but that's our strategy, that's our plan. Coming right down from the Pentagon and the Oval Office. Just keep driving those freakin' roads. It's the stupidity, Ramona. The utter stupidity."

He stopped talking and stared at his milk glass. Beads of sweat dotted his forehead.

Ramona reached out to squeeze his forearm. She lifted the milk carton, topped off his glass, then placed an Oreo on his napkin. "It's okay, babe. You're safe here with me." Tears filled her eyes. She did her best to blink them back.

12

An old warehouse on the north edge of town had been converted into the home of Foothill Batting Cages. Step inside on a busy day and you'd be greeted by the ping of aluminum bats connecting with hard rubber balls fired by a half-dozen pitching machines. Space had also been set aside for a couple of bullpens where pitchers could train. The lobby area included a snack bar and two rooms that could be rented for birthday parties and team celebrations. On a mid-week afternoon in March, the place was dead quiet.

Two young men stepped through the front door and checked with the attendant at the counter. He directed them to one of the party rooms and they made their way, carrying equipment bags stuffed with baseball gear.

Webb Johnson waited inside, checking his watch, anxious to meet Brett Corcoran and get started. The door opened and the young men entered.

"Mr. Johnson?" The tall one with the sandy hair and intense blue eyes approached and extended his hand. "Hi, I'm Brett Corcoran." He turned to his shorter, dark-haired companion. "This is Joey DiFranco. Everybody calls him Joey D."

"Brett. Joey D." Webb shook hands with both of them. "Just call me Webb."

Brett continued. "Joey D has agreed to be my bullpen catcher, in exchange for me throwing batting practice to him. He's an outfielder trying to make the GRCC team. We've been workout partners for a while."

"Joey D, I'm glad to have you as a bullpen catcher. I sure as hell can't do it anymore."

"Nice to meet you, Mr. Johnson...I mean Webb."

Webb led them to the side of the room where three folding chairs were open in front of a large whiteboard. "We've got about thirty minutes until our reserved bullpen time. I thought I'd give Brett a quick rundown about what we're going to be working on."

Brett and Joey D sat down while Webb picked up a dry erase pen and began. "Brett...as a pitcher you have three tools to work with."

"You mean, like, fastball, curveball, changeup?"

"No, son. Step back a little bit, think elemental." Webb wrote on the whiteboard.

VELOCITY
LOCATION
MOVEMENT

"You master those three tools and you could be standing on the mound at Oracle Park." Webb stood quietly, letting the message sink in.

Brett frowned. "I've got velocity. Plenty of it."

"You've got a good strong arm, son. But velocity isn't just about throwin' hard. It's about changin' speeds, messin' with the hitters' timing." Webb watched Brett's expression. Was he going to buy in? "But we're gonna work on velocity another day. Today, I want to focus on location."

Two equipment bags with the name Johnson stenciled in white sat on the floor near the whiteboard. Webb went to one of them and pulled out a tall, thin paperback book, the pages yellowed and dog-eared. The title on the front page read, *The Science of Hitting*,

by Ted Williams. Webb pulled a chair in front of Brett, sat down and handed him the book.

"What's this? *The Science of Hitting*? I'm a pitcher, Mr. Johnson. I seldom ever get to hit."

Webb laughed. "Look at the cover, son."

Brett stared at a full-page cover shot of Ted Williams in his famous left-handed batting stance, accompanied by a diagram of the strike zone. Superimposed on the zone were an array of baseballs, seven baseballs wide, eleven high. Each ball was inscribed with a batting average.

"The point Mr. Williams is making is pretty simple. 'Get a good pitch to hit.' If the pitcher hits that low outside spot down there," he said, pointing at the chart, "Ted says he would likely hit .230. Remember, this is a lifetime .344 hitter, probably the greatest that ever played the game. Now look up here, toward the middle of the zone. Pitches in that area, he's saying he could hit .400." Webb paused again.

"Okay...I get that." Brett glanced at Joey D who was soaking it up like a Bible lesson.

"The message for you, Brett, is you got to pitch to those spots the hitter hates. You got to keep your pitches out of a hitter's happy zone." Another pause. "That's a big part of 'location.' There's more, but Mr. Ted Williams's chart is a good place to start. That's where we're gonna begin today, work on hitting spots."

Brett looked up and nodded.

Webb was pleased. *So far, so good. As least he listened.*

13

The Hotel Truro was an historic landmark in the heart of Gold Ridge. It dated from the time of the 49ers and was named for the cathedral city in Cornwall in honor of the Cornish immigrants who settled the area to work in the mines. It was the oldest continuously operating hotel in the Mother Lode and boasted a fine dining room that featured continental cuisine. An elegant private room was set aside for hosting special events and on a chilly March night, ten men and women gathered for a festive meal.

Don Corcoran was the host for the evening, pulling out all the stops to entertain six guests representing a prospective client. The evening began with cocktails and appetizers, followed by a *prix fixe* meal featuring a different wine for each course. The *sommelier* hovered close, reviewing each choice with the host, presenting the cork, pouring a splash into a fresh glass for approval. Don was in his element. If this evening did not close the deal, nothing would.

As the dessert course was served—mixed berries with fresh zabaglione—he launched into a favorite story, his voice rising from the head of the table. All eyes turned in his direction.

"So, it was eighteen years ago that I interviewed for a job with The Sherman Group. I made it through a couple of levels and then found myself face to face with Old Mac." The guests smiled, knowing Old

Mac referred to company founder and CEO, MacKenzie Sherman. "Old Mac looks at me and says, 'Mr. Corcoran, what do you know about erp?' Well, I knew E-R-P stood for Enterprise Resource Planning and it was the company's primary software product, but that's all I knew. I had a brain freeze right there in front of The Man. He didn't say a word, just let me sit there like the proverbial deer in the headlights. I knew I had to say something, or I was out of there and back on the street. I said, 'Well, sir, here's what I know about Earp. There were six or seven Earp siblings—Wyatt, Morgan, Virgil, James—but for the life of me I can't remember the rest of those Earps.'" The group around the table roared with laughter. Don waited, soaking it up, playing the moment for all it was worth, until it was time to deliver the punchline. "Old Mac nearly fell out of his chair laughing…and hired me on the spot!"

Another round of laughter filled the room as coffee cups were refilled. Don suggested cognac, but the guests had reached their limit of alcohol. Fortunately, the prospective clients were booked into rooms at the hotel and did not have to venture out for a drive home. That left The Sherman Group employees to fend for themselves. Though Don was "in his cups," he had the presence of mind to call cabs and get his colleagues home safely. He placed his company credit card in the black leather folder that held the check and staggered to his feet. It was time to say goodnight to his guests.

MacKenzie Sherman stood behind his desk and looked out the window of his office. From the fourth floor, looking east, there was a fine view of the historic downtown district, and beyond, the mighty snowcapped Sierra Nevada range. He was a short, heavyset man with snow white hair, fond of wearing three-piece suits and fine silk ties. He was waiting for his Vice President of Marketing to arrive, thinking through the message he wanted to deliver. This would be

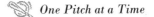

the proverbial "come to Jesus" meeting. The message would not be pleasant.

The Sherman Group was a local success story, founded two decades earlier as a software development firm with a handful of employees. Today it was considered a powerhouse in the marketplace, its flagship ERP software propagating to firms large and small throughout the western states. The application suite was known as GenSys (for General Systems) and the current iteration was cloud-based, giving Sherman's clients infinite flexibility and pricing that scaled to their needs. Old Mac, as he was affectionately known, was the sole proprietor. He had resisted the urge to go public, loath to cede control to a board of directors, or succumb to stockholder pressure for short term profits. MacKenzie Sherman, as could be expected, was fierce in protecting his company. No one could be allowed to sully the reputation of The Sherman Group.

There was a soft knock on the massive oak door. Old Mac turned and spoke in a firm tenor. "Come in."

The door opened and Don Corcoran entered. "Good afternoon, sir. You wanted to see me?"

"Yes, Don. Have a seat." He motioned toward a chair in front of his desk. His own chair was a high-backed leather behemoth that seemed to tower over anyone who sat on the other side of the desk. Sherman took his seat and locked eyes with Don Corcoran.

"I understand you entertained a prospective client at the Truro last Friday night."

"Yes, sir."

"I've been in contact with the president of the company and I don't like what I'm hearing."

"Oh…really?"

"I hear you were loud, obnoxious, intoxicated. Should I go on?"

"Sir, I don't think anyone was intoxicated. We'd had a very productive day presenting our product, and I wanted to entertain them in style, as we have with many other clients."

Old Mac was quiet for a moment. "Look, Don, I know the clients expect to be wined and dined, and I'm aware of the book of business you've won for the company..."

"Yes, sir?"

"...but I will not tolerate public drunkenness. No employee is going to embarrass our firm, no matter his or her title."

"I understand, sir."

The old man continued, his voice softer now. "Don, I know you suffered a terrible loss four years ago. I was very fond of Joanne, you know that. She was a lovely person..."

"Yes, sir."

"...and you've been here for—what is it now—eighteen years?"

"Eighteen years. Yes, sir.'

"I'm going to cut you some slack, but not much. Trust me on this. If I hear any more reports of this kind, you'll be back in here to turn in your badge and your keys. Is that clear?"

"Yes, it is, Mr. Sherman."

Sherman stood and walked around his desk. He clapped Don on the shoulder and led him to the massive oak door. "Don, let me ask you point blank. Do you have a drinking problem?"

"No, sir. I enjoy a drink at the end of the day, but I don't have a problem with it."

"The company is behind you if you need help, Don. I think you've earned it. Just say the word."

"Thank you, sir. I appreciate your being frank with me." The two men shook hands.

Don's hands continued to shake as he left the office.

14

April 25, 2019

Crusty's Corner

I finished reading the Mueller Report today, all four hundred some-odd pages. My initial reaction is, *I'd like to see what's behind all those redaction bars.* That will likely be for future generations.

In Volume I of the report, Muller concludes there was no *conspiracy*. Notice I didn't say *collusion.* There sure were a lot of contacts with Russian persons, but no evidence of conspiracy. That is if you completely ignore the June 2016 Trump Tower meeting with a clown car full of Russians, plus Donald Trump Jr., Jared Kushner, and Paul Manafort.

As I read it, the Russians said they had dirt on Hillary Clinton. That was the *quid.* In return, if Trump were elected, they wanted to see some troublesome sanctions lifted. That was the *pro quo.*

Don Jr. was ready to play, but for one problem. The Russians didn't bring the dirt. In most clandestine deals, the seller brings a taste to prove the quality of the goods. And so, Don Jr., Jared, and Paul walked away empty handed. No deal.

Subsequently, Don Sr., with help from his merry band of minstrels, concocted a lie. The meeting was about Russian adoptions. Yeah, right.

Volume II takes up the question of obstruction of justice. Mueller's team documents in excruciating detail eleven instances that could be construed as obstruction. The bigees (my opinion) are Trump's attempts to have Mueller removed, engaging White House Counsel Don McGhan to assist in that effort, then directing McGhan to falsify the record and hide his tracks.

Ultimately, Mueller declined to issue charges. The reasoning goes like this: a sitting president cannot be indicted; therefore, to charge without the benefit of an indictment and subsequent trial would deny the president a chance to defend himself. The constitutional remedy is impeachment, which can only be taken up by Congress. In other words, *There ya go, Congress. The ball's in your court.*

My copy of the Mueller Report includes Attorney General William Barr's four-page summary released on March 24. I'm having a hard time reconciling Barr's summary with the actual report. Were we deliberately mislead? Was the Barr summary just air cover so that President Trump could declare complete exoneration? After all, we would not see the report itself for several weeks. By then, would anyone take time to read the damn thing?

As the saying goes, it is what it is. One thing is crystal clear: President Trump has found his Roy Cohn.

—R.Q. Crutchfeld

15

It was one thing for Webb Johnson to say, *do this, do that.* It was something else altogether to make it happen. Lessons are hard to implement, especially from sixty feet six inches. Brett spent two weeks on the mound at Foothill Batting Cages learning to hit spots in and around the strike zone. At first, he had to sacrifice velocity. His average fastball dropped two to three miles per hour, but it all came back as he gained concentration and confidence. At the final planned bullpen session, everything came together. *Glove side, knees.* Pop! *Arm side, shoulders.* Pop! *Eye level, just above the zone.* Pop! Brett was thrilled, Webb was smiling, and Joey D's glove hand was red and swollen.

"What's next, Coach?" The pupil was grinning ear to ear.

"We're gonna talk about velocity. It's time you learned a changeup."

Brett couldn't wait for the next lesson. "Easy peasy, Webb."

Work on a changeup began on a Monday. By Wednesday, Brett was ready to quit.

"Goddamn it, Webb. I'm trying my best. I just can't do it. It doesn't feel right."

"Okay, let's go over it again. It's called a circle change. Start with the grip, like this, your thumb and forefinger touching, the ball back in your palm a little. The ball is going to come off the last three fingers, like this." Webb approved Brett's grip. "Remember, the key is to keep everything else the same. Same rock and kick, same stride, same arm speed. The only difference is the grip. Okay, let's try again."

Bret went into his windup, drove toward the plate, released the ball and watched as it bounced four feet in front of home plate. He bent over, hands on his knees, and stared at the ground. The session continued and so did the abysmal results. Brett's frustration was reaching the boiling point. Another attempt bounced wide and far left of the plate.

"Let's try again." Webb said, in a calm, measured voice.

For Brett, it sounded like *Pass the potatoes.* It was the final straw, the one that reached the breaking point. He threw down his glove, put on his jacket, and stormed out of the building.

Webb looked at Joey D and shrugged. They began to stuff their equipment bags. It was time to head for home.

"Let him chill, Joey D. I'll call you when he's ready for the next session."

"You think he'll come back, Webb?"

"Brett's not a quitter. No sir. No quit in that boy."

"Got to admit, Webb, that temper scares me sometimes."

"He's seeing a counselor at the VA. He's workin' on it. Let's give him some space."

Joey D held the door for the old coach as they went out into the cold. Webb wasn't nearly as confident as his words.

The trio assembled for the next session one week later, allegedly ready to work. Webb had a new wrinkle to try, but he wanted to judge the weather first.

"Ready to give it the ol' college try, young man?" Webb's tone was light, teasing.

"Yeah, Coach. Ready to go."

"Did you have one of them epiphanies?"

"You could say that." Brett smiled. "I had a talk with Ramona."

"And?" Webb couldn't wait to hear the answer.

"She told me I had to listen to you and do whatever you say."

"Or?"

"Or else I'd be taking showers by myself." Brett's cheeks turned bright red.

"Well, there ya go. Smart girl!" The old man laughed out loud. "Let's get after it."

Webb's new wrinkle was actually an old one, pulled from his bag of coaching tricks. Brett and Joey D would simply play catch, backing up a step or two with each throw, until they reached ninety feet. From there, Brett would take his windup and throw with about seventy percent effort, make a good, firm throw and hit Joey D in the chest. The wrinkle was he had to alternate grips—four-seam fastball, then circle change. This modified long-toss was intended to imbed the feeling of keeping everything the same, except for the grip.

"Think like Einstein, Brett. E equals MC squared. We're only changing one variable and that variable is C."

"Shit, Webb!" Brett couldn't suppress a laugh. "I'm no physics major, but that doesn't make a damn bit of sense."

Webb broke up laughing and Joey D joined in. It was a nice break in the tension.

By the following Wednesday, Brett had the mechanics mastered. By Friday, he could take it to the mound and mix the changeup into his bullpen work. The new pitch wasn't finished, but it was on its way.

"You're a genius, Coach!" Brett blurted as they walked to the exit.

Webb smiled. *You got that right, son.* He kept it to himself.

16

Ramona could not sleep. She wished Brett were there to hold her, safe and warm and well-loved, while she fell asleep. But he was working late, something about inventory being taken at Big 5. She tossed and turned and pressed the button on her cell phone to display the time. It was 2:54 a.m. Maybe a glass of water, or better yet, a glass of milk. No, that would make her want to pee. The problem was in her head, fears and doomsday scenarios playing on an endless loop.

She needed to call her parents in Roseville, hadn't spoken to them for a few days. Were they okay? Were they worried? Were they afraid? Ramona thought of the night she confronted her parents in the kitchen of their modest three-bedroom home. Why were they constantly huddled at the table, talking in hushed tones? What was going on? She demanded to know. After all, she was sixteen, an adult. If there was a problem, she had a right to be informed. Her mother's tears did not stifle her demands. Her father finally told her to take a seat, be quiet, and listen.

"Your mother and I came to this country illegally when you were a baby. In Matamoros, I was a journalist, your mother was a nurse. I became the target of the Gulf Cartel because of things that I wrote. We had no choice but to flee. My brother, your uncle Fred, had immigrated legally years before. He and Aunt Imelda took us in, I went to work in his construction business, and Mama, as you know, found work as a caregiver. Uncle Fred took care of everything, all the necessary documentation, all the required bribes, and we just blended into the community, just like citizens."

Ramona's father continued, the worry lines cutting deep into his forehead.

"Today there is an uproar over immigration. They say more than ten or twelve million are here illegally. There is pressure to make most if not all return to Mexico or wherever and wait their turn to come legally. And that includes you, my daughter, who has known no other country, who is as American as Barack Obama."

She remembered the tears in her father's eyes. She had never seen him cry, not ever. That was six years ago, and though they had moved on with their lives, as though nothing was wrong, sleep became a problem for Ramona. What if the authorities found out? Would they come and take her parents away, deport them to Matamoros? And what of her plans for school and her dream of becoming a nurse? Would they send her away too? Of course they would! And now there is this man Trump who speaks of nothing but walls and gangs and rapists and murderers. And, oh God in heaven, how she wished Brett were there to keep the demons away.

Ramona knew she had to tell him she was illegal. She was in love with him, and he with her. She was sure of that. And it was way past time for keeping secrets. Brett was a good, kind, beautiful man, and none of it would matter to him.

Would it?

She checked her phone again. It was 3:05 a.m. A key rattled in the front door lock. Brett was home! She threw back the covers and ran to him, leaping into his arms, sobbing against his chest.

"Whoa! Hey, what is it, baby? What's wrong? It's okay. It's okay now. I'm here. I'm home…"

17

In the town of Gold Ridge, if someone suggested Mexican food, there was only one sure choice, a place on the east side called Rosalita's. It was a family-run business with three generations busy onsite most days of the week, a place that crackled with positive energy and festive cheer. The restaurant's name honored the matriarch of the Montero family, and Rosalita herself, though now in her eighties, was a constant presence. She wandered by the tables and booths, greeting her loyal customers, making sure her recipes had been executed perfectly.

Ramona Hernandez loved waiting tables at Rosalita's. She felt like an honorary member of the family.

The dinner crowd filled the restaurant, every table occupied, people waiting on the sidewalk outside, hoping to get in. Brett Corcoran and Webb Johnson relaxed in a vinyl-covered booth and enjoyed cold drinks—Dos Equis for Brett, Pepsi for Webb—with chips and salsa. Ramona had taken their orders and hurried away to the kitchen.

"What's up with your girl, Brett? Doesn't seem herself tonight." Webb dipped a warm chip into the spicy salsa.

"She's got a lot on her mind, Webb. We'll be okay."

Webb noted the plural *we,* but he didn't pursue it. "Gotta tell you, son, she is special! Smart, hard workin', kind. She's got a heart full of love. Question is, what the hell does she see in you?"

Brett laughed and took a long pull on his beer. "Never question a lucky streak, Webb. You know that." He waved away a Mariachi trio that had strolled up to their booth. "So, Coach, what's your take? How are we doing?"

"I think we're okay. You've learned to appreciate location, at least with your fastball. You're making great progress on velocity, especially how to change speeds. The changeup is coming along nicely. I'd say we're doin' pretty good."

"So, what's next, Webb?"

"Good question. We've gotta start talking about movement, which is a hell of a topic."

"Yeah?"

"Yeah. Watching your old tapes, I can see you have no breaking pitch, not even a clue. You need to learn a curveball, or a slider, something that moves sharply. That's part of it."

"Okay."

"And we need to work on adding movement to your fastball. You've got good velocity, mid-nineties, but it's straight. There are ways to add movement." Webb paused to sip his cola. "The good news is your changeup has movement. It drops real nice at the tail end. So, that's a good start."

Brett smiled, obviously pleased with Webb's assessment. Webb saw the smile and threw cold water on it.

"Don't get too cocky, kid. What's comin' up is damn hard. You think learning the changeup was a pain? That was nothin' compared to what's ahead."

Ramona approached their table, a large platter balanced on one hand, a folding stand in the other. She opened the stand and placed the tray with the smooth, practiced motion of a professional. "Okay, boys. Here ya go. Rosalita's famous combo plates. Knock yourselves out."

Webb reached out and took her hand. "Honey, even if the food here was bad, which it ain't, I'd still come in just to see you."

She grabbed his drink and threatened to pour the dark liquid on his head, laughing as she did so. Webb caught Brett's eye, saw he was laughing too, and made it unanimous. It was a beautiful thing to share.

18

June 28, 2019

Crusty's Corner

Kamala Harris took a swing at Joe Biden last night and landed a serious blow. She pointed to Biden's opposition to school busing in the 1970s, spoke of a little girl bused across town in Berkeley, California, and said, "That little girl was me."

Much of the oxygen left the room.

Biden tried to recover stating school integration via busing was a decision to be made by local school districts, not at the Federal level. Harris pushed back, saying this is where the Federal government needs to step in.

As a resident of the East Bay at the time in question, I'm inclined to say both Harris and Biden are right.

Here's why: Berkeley of 1970s presented an uncommon, if not unique, situation. People of color tended to live in the flatlands, with I-80 and San Francisco Bay forming the western border.

Wealthier residents lived in neighborhoods further east, rising into the hills.

Busing kids out of the flatlands to integrate schools in affluent neighborhoods required a very short ride, generally less than five miles.

U.C. Berkeley was also a major influence, a liberal-leaning community that had strongly supported the civil rights movement. Faced with school integration, it was time to put up or shut up: did the community have the courage of its convictions? It most assuredly did.

My point is Berkeley was the ideal place to try school integration via busing. And for the most part, it worked out well. Witness Senator Kamala Harris.

Former Vice President Biden is also right: one size does not fit all. Not every community has the confluence of circumstances to make busing a viable option. The decision should be made at the local level—unless or until it becomes clear a district's goal is to maintain segregation.

That said, I see no reason Senator Harris and Vice President Biden can't hug and make up. And thanks for a lively debate, what we used to call *Must See TV.*

—R.Q. Crutchfeld

19

The office was stuffy on a warm June day, the air conditioning vent putting out a weak stream of cool air. Brett provided Dr. Michael Bowman with a recap of the events of the past two weeks. Bowman listened, jotting notes on his steno pad.

What the hell is he writing? Wish I could see his damn notes. Brett continued his monologue, rambling on with no particular direction.

Bowman interrupted. "Brett, let's talk about Iraq."

"What about it?"

"I know just a few details about what happened, about your convoy being attacked. That was in your second tour over there, right?"

"Yeah."

"What can you tell me about that day?"

Brett saw red spots flash across his field of vision. "Oh sure, I could tell you…but you really had to be there. Know what I mean?" He felt bad about the blurted sarcasm, but only for a moment. *These damn counselors should do a tour of duty in a combat zone.*

Bowman didn't flinch. "Help me out, Brett. Tell me about your mission that day."

Brett felt a jolt, as though someone hit him with a cattle prod. "Mission? You want to know the mission? What freakin' mission?

There was no mission. I mean, go way back to the beginning. What was the mission then? Weapons of Mass Destruction. WMDs. We were gonna take down Saddam and destroy all his WMDs. How did that mission turn out, huh? Oh, right. There were no WMDs.

"So, now what's the mission? Democracy! We're gonna bring democracy to the Iraqi people, from the U.S. of A. with love. Did you ask for any of this? Hell no, but you're getting it anyway. We're gonna pour billions of dollars on you and you're gonna love it. And if ninety-nine percent of you never see a goddamn dime, well, that's the way it's done. And if some of you don't like it, we'll keep kicking your asses until you get in line. We'll do midnight raids and terrify your families. We'll lock people in Abu Ghraib and treat them like animals. And we'll bring firepower like you've never seen. Talk about MWDs—wait till you see what we bring.

"Mission? Mission, my ass! Look, doc, there's only one *real* mission when you're deployed there. Stay alive. Fight for your brothers and sisters. Keep *them* alive. Do whatever it takes, regardless of what the command says. Every warrior we send home alive is a victory, and a spit-in-the-face to the cocksuckers who sent us there. *That's* the mission!"

Dr. Bowman was quiet. He flipped the pages of his steno pad where he'd scribbled furiously while Brett spoke. He dropped the pad on his desk and locked eyes with Brett.

"Okay. I think we made real progress today. Our time's about up. Will I see you next week?"

Brett was dumbstruck. *That's it? That's all you've got?* He rose from the chair, gave the doctor a mock salute, and left the office.

20

Small towns have a unique quality. It feels as if you know everyone and they know you and people look out for one another. The connections are strong, formed in schools, youth activities, civic organizations, local businesses, and especially houses of worship.

Police officers in a small town play an important role. They see the townsfolk at their very best and their absolute worst, and there are few secrets. For the most part, sworn officers are *of* the community. When they take off their uniforms, they become scout troop leaders, Little League coaches, Sunday school teachers, and the first ones called when a volunteer is needed for a worthy cause. Most take seriously the ideal, "To protect and serve." And so, it was no anomaly when Officer Ted Zane picked up the phone at Police headquarters and called Lilly Morgan.

Lilly lunged for the phone as soon as it rang. Don was late and she was worried.

"Hello?"

"Lilly, hi! This is Ted Zane. How are you?"

She recognized the voice and the name, an officer with the Gold Ridge Police Department and a member of the church she attended.

"Hi, Ted. I'm good. What's up?" She frowned and took a quick breath. *How rude. I didn't even ask how he was.*

"Lilly, I've got Don down here at the station. My partner and I stopped him over on Third Street, driving erratically."

"Oh my God! Is he okay?"

"Yeah, he's fine, just sitting out in the squad room, cooling his heels. Had a few too many is all."

"Oh Lord. Ted...are you going to book him?" Lilly's mind began to race through the impacts of a DUI arrest.

"No. That's why I'm calling. I didn't give him a test or anything. Just had him park his vehicle and lock it up, brought him down here and called you."

"Oh, Ted. Thank you, thank you so much."

"Hey, it's nothing, Lilly. You're good people. No need to go nuclear over something like this." Ted paused. "As long as it doesn't happen again."

"Believe me, Ted, I'll make sure it doesn't. Let me grab my coat and purse and I'll be there in a few minutes. And, Ted..."

"Yeah?"

"I can't tell how grateful I am...how grateful *we* are."

"Okay, Lilly. See you in a few."

Officer Zane could have played it by the book: a breathalyzer test, an arrest for driving under the influence, a night in the city jail, court appearances, a stiff fine, suspended license, and so on. But these were people he knew, people he bowed his head and prayed with most Sundays. Ted Zane's concept of "protect and serve" had room for compassion and second chances.

As long as it didn't happen again.

Lilly retraced her route, heading home, Don slumped in the passenger seat next to her. Strange that she thought of it as *home* because none of it belonged to her. Lilly and Don's son Brett had been engaged in a slow-motion shift, Brett gradually moving in with Ramona, and Lilly filling the empty space in Don's house. It was an awkward situation, half of her things in her apartment across town, the other half stored here and there at Don's. In one sense, this was good. She could leave at any time if things went bad, and she'd seen this drinking issue coming on, like a slow-moving freight train. She could just say *enough*, pack up and leave, and no one would blame her. It would be easy, except for the fact that she loved the man.

"Don, for God's sake, what were you thinking?"

"Geez, Lilly, calm down. I just went out with some of guys after work. Just a couple of beers."

"Sure, just a couple. You reek, Don! Like a skid row bum."

"Oh, come on—"

"Do you realize what a DUI means? How do you think Mac Sherman would react? Huh? Answer that?"

She was shouting at him while trying to focus on the road. He did not answer her questions. They rode the rest of way in silence.

Conventional wisdom holds that the best thing for a drunk is to fill him or her with black coffee, as if it were a magic elixir capable of curing the problem. The process results in a wide-awake drunk, probably one with a queasy stomach, ready to vomit the entire load. Maybe that's the true remedy: void the stomach, stop the absorption of alcohol. But then, why coffee? Why not castor oil?

When they arrived at the house nestled among the pines, Lilly sent Don to take a shower while she collected the clothes he'd been wearing—a suit, dress shirt and tie—and stuffed them in a bag to go to the cleaners. She went into the kitchen and brewed a pot of strong coffee, adding an extra scoop for effect. Don entered the kitchen in a dark bathrobe, his hair wet and slicked back.

Lilly's anger had subsided, replaced by immense concern. "Look, Don, this cannot go on. You have to do something…*we* have to do something…to get your drinking under control."

"I know, I know. You're right, honey—" Don sounded contrite.

"And don't just call me 'honey' and tell me what I want to hear. We are way past that."

"Okay, okay. I got it. I'll stop, right now, tonight. Empty the liquor cabinet, get it out of the house, I'm through as of now."

"How about professional help?"

"I can do this, Lilly. I can lick it on my own." He hesitated. The words that followed seemed caught in his throat. "I promise you."

He looked away from her eyes and drank the bitter coffee.

21

There is a coffee company in the town of Gold Ridge known far and wide for its custom roasts. The little company calls itself The Magic Bean and its shop is crowded throughout the day with locals and day trippers up from the valley, dropping in to enjoy a favorite barista creation, or to purchase beans for brewing at home.

Webb Johnson secured a small table by the window and waited, enjoying a large latte'. Don Corcoran entered the shop, waved, and went to stand in the order line. With a tall insulated cup in hand, Don approached the table.

"Hey, Webb. How's it going?"

"It's all good, man. Thanks for taking the time to meet with me."

"No problem. You said you had a request, but first, bring me up to date. How is Brett doing?"

"It's a mixed bag, Don, but mostly good. He's got a good handle on location and velocity, and now we're working on movement. It's not an easy thing, but we're changing his arm slot, where he releases the ball, dropping it down a little to three-quarters."

"Yeah, how's that going over?"

"He's picked it up really well and it's created nice movement on his four-seam fastball. I have him working on a two-seam fastball, which he's never thrown before, and it's coming along. His two-seamer has nice sink to it."

"Sounds good, but you said it was mixed." Don held eye contact while he removed the plastic lid from his coffee.

"Yeah, the arm slot change, the two-seamer—that's the good news. The bad news is we're still trying to find a breaking pitch that works for him. Tried a slider, tried a curveball, tried a cutter. It's been a struggle and he's gettin' frustrated. I'm giving him a few days off to regroup. You know how anger gets the best of him. I don't want to push too hard."

Don removed a small silver flask from the inside breast pocket of his suit and held it below the table to unscrew the top. He took his coffee cup below the table and poured in a shot from the flask.

"What the hell are you doin'?" Webb looked at him in shock. "It's frickin' 8:30 in the morning and you're spikin' your damn coffee?"

"Hey, keep your voice down, Webb. Just a little pick-me-up, that's all. You said you had a request."

"Wait just a damn minute. What's in the flask?"

"Brandy. That's all. Like I said, a little morning booster."

"Man, there is a fine English word that fits you like a tee. You, my friend, are a hypocrite. You tell me I have to dry out to work with your son, and you sit here pouring brandy in your mornin' coffee."

"Yeah, well, I notice you are still cashing my checks, Coach." *Coach* sounded like a four-letter word. "Now, are you going to tell me your request or not?"

The words stung and Webb was quiet for a moment. He decided to let it go—for now. "Yeah, okay, here's what I need. I want to use your camcorder to film Brett's bullpen sessions. Should have been doin' it all along. I want him to see his arm slot, see all the pitches coming from the same place. I'll need a tripod, too."

"Okay. You got it."

"Also, a small flat screen that I can hook the camera to, so Brett can replay a session right there in the bullpen."

"That too, no problem." Don made notes on a napkin with a ballpoint pen. "Is that it?"

Webb looked at Don. Concern overwhelmed him. "Sorry to go all righteous on you, man. Listen, I'm hooked up with an AA group here in town. They meet in the basement at the old Methodist church. I can connect you with a sponsor. That is, if you are ready to get help."

"I've got it handled, Webb. But thanks for your concern." Don stuffed the napkin in his pocket. "I'll let you know when I have these things together for you. Okay? And thanks for everything you're doing for Brett." He turned and looked toward the door. "I've got to get back to work."

Webb watched Don walk away with his special coffee in hand. He shook his head and mumbled to himself. *Poor dumb bastard.*

22

It was a forty-five-minute drive from Gold Ridge to Roseville. Or at least it should be, depending on traffic through the city of Auburn. A few miles west on Interstate 80, near Newcastle, one hits the crest of a ridge and the great Sacramento Valley comes into view. The freeway extends in a perfectly straight line toward the skyline of Sacramento. Beyond the capital city, off to the west, the Coast Range rises in deep blue shadow. The sweeping view—north, west, and south—takes in one of the richest agricultural valleys in the world.

Brett rode in the passenger seat of Ramona's six-year-old Honda Civic as they topped the ridge, on their way to visit her parents.

"Wow!" He caught his breath. "That view always blows me away. It's good to get out of the hills once in a while."

"Yeah. I need to see my folks more often. It's just been so busy, getting ready for finals, working."

"Very proud of you, babe. Just one more year, you'll be taking your exam to become a Registered Nurse."

Ramona did not respond.

Brett glanced her way. "You okay?"

"Yeah. I'm just worried about my parents. I can tell they are frightened. ICE has been active in their area, doing raids at four in the morning, crap like that. They know people who have been arrested and deported. They're scared, Brett."

"I can't blame them. But what about you? They could come after you, too."

"Believe me, I've thought about it. That's what keeps me awake at night."

Brett paused, then posed a question he'd been holding. "Ramona, did you ever consider DACA? The DACA people are protected for the time being at least."

"We talked about it—Mom and Dad and I—but I was afraid if I went to register for DACA, it would make my parents a target. So, I didn't go." She frowned. "It's really weird. I have a birth certificate that says I was born here. I have a Social Security Card. I file my tax returns on time every year. I feel like a citizen."

"And your parents?"

"They have all the documentation, too. Just good, hard-working, tax-paying citizens. What worries me is how many people know we're here illegally? There's my aunt and uncle, of course. But who else? Where did our documents come from? And what about family back in Mexico? Do they know our status? You know what they say—if more than one person knows your secret, it isn't a secret anymore."

Brett rubbed her knee and tried to reassure her. But he knew she was right. There had to be a solution, probably something involving an attorney. The thought caused a knot in his stomach. He tried another subject. "Are you worried about your folks meeting me? I'm sure they weren't hoping for a blonde, blue-eyed Irishman."

Ramona laughed. "That's the least of my worries right now. Besides, they'll love you once they get to know you. Just be your handsome, charming self."

They drove in silence down from the foothills, through the rolling countryside turned light brown by the summer sun. Ramona took the Atlantic Street exit and wound through the streets of Roseville, tracing the familiar route to her parents' home in the old neighborhood near Roseville High.

"There's my high school," she said, as they drove past the sprawling campus. "I was a cheerleader. Go Tigers!"

~~~

The tidy three-bedroom home sat well back from the sidewalk, fronted by a neatly trimmed lawn. The stucco walls were a warm beige, the trim a dark chocolate brown, and the paint looked fresh. Ramona's parents greeted her with lingering hugs, followed by polite handshakes for Brett. Ramona and her mother, Consuelo, went directly to the kitchen where dinner was on the stove while her father and Brett settled in the living room with tall glasses of iced tea.

Paul Hernandez was of medium height, about five nine, with a slim build and sharp features. His short black hair was graying at the temples and Brett guessed he was in his late fifties. Conversation was stiff in the beginning and Brett noted that Mr. Hernandez did not like talking about himself, finding ways to turn the conversation toward other topics.

"Ramona tells me you are in construction, Mr. Hernandez."

"Please call me Paul. Yes, I am a foreman with my brother Fred's company. But tell me, Brett, I understand you play baseball, that you are an accomplished pitcher."

"Well, not so accomplished, sir. But yes, I am a pitcher. I had success in high school but left the game for about three years. Now I'm working with a coach, trying to get back into it."

"And why did you stop playing?"

"I enlisted in the Army. Did two tours in Iraq."

"Oh…thank God you're back in one piece." Paul smiled.

Brett sipped his iced tea and tried to change the subject. "So, I saw a lot of building going on as we drove down today. Must be a good time for your business?"

"Yes, it is. Very busy, knock wood." He rapped his knuckles on the table next to his chair. "Tell me about this coach you are working with. What are your goals, your next steps?"

73

There it was again, the quick change of subject. There were things neither of them wanted to talk about. Brett decided to go with the flow.

"Well, I plan to enroll at Gold Ridge Community College and win a spot on the baseball team. The local colleges are well scouted, by four-year schools and the pros. A contract with a major league team would be my first choice. If not, a scholarship offer to a good college program would allow me to continue playing and developing." Brett dropped the modesty. "One way or another, Paul, I am going to play professional baseball."

Paul smiled. "I admire your confidence. A man must believe in himself. Am I right?"

"Yes, sir, Mr. Hernandez!"

"And is there a Plan B?"

"Sir?"

"Do you have a backup plan in case a professional career doesn't happen for you?"

Ramona came into the living room. "Okay, gentlemen, dinner is served."

Brett left the question hanging in the air as he took his seat at the dining room table. They joined hands and Paul offered grace.

"Heavenly Father, bless this food that it may nourish our bodies to serve thee better. And we ask that you bless our new friend Brett and our beloved Ramona as they pursue their dreams. In Jesus's name we pray. Amen."

Brett blinked back tears and reached for his water glass. He could not remember ever being blessed, though it must have happened at some point in his life. He managed to make the sign of the cross and say, "Amen."

Consuelo Hernandez had prepared a feast. There were beans and rice, of course, but handmade tamales, chili relleno, and deep-fried chicken taquitos were the stars of the meal.

Brett leaned close to Ramona and whispered, "Better than Rosalita's."

Ramona laughed. "Mom, Brett says your food is better than Rosalita's."

"And who is this Rosalita? Some young pup? What does she know?"

The conversation around the table touched many topics and Brett was impressed with Paul and Consuelo—informed, articulate, passionate in their opinions. The roots of Ramona's intelligence were clear.

After a delicious flan for dessert, it was time to say goodbye and begin the long drive to Gold Ridge. Brett accepted a warm embrace from Consuelo, then turned to Paul.

"It was wonderful meeting you, sir. Thanks for everything." He didn't say it, but the thought was clear in his mind. *I'll be thinking about Plan B.*

23

There are few things more annoying than a loose handle on the silverware drawer in the kitchen. At least not to Lilly Morgan. She'd been after Don to take a screwdriver to it and stop the annoyance, but somehow, he never found time. There is an old saying: *If you want something done right, do it yourself.* She decided it was time.

Lilly went into the garage and found Don's toolbox on a shelf below his workbench. She lifted the box to the surface of the bench and opened the latch. Inside, tucked neatly on top, was a half-empty pint of vodka. Lilly's heart dropped. *Okay, benefit of the doubt. Maybe this was before he took the pledge. Don't jump to conclusions.*

What other hiding places were there in the garage? She looked around and saw his golf bag in the corner against the wall. Did she dare look through the many compartments? Would that violate Don's privacy? Lilly had to know. She went to the bag and zipped open the various pockets. On the left side, down among scuffed golf balls and broken tees, was another bottle, *Smirnoff* glaring in bright red letters across the label. Tears welled in her eyes. How many more bottles were there, and how hard did she want to search? Don would not be home for a couple of hours. She had plenty of time.

The tires of Don's BMW crunched the gravel driveway. Lilly filled two tall glasses with ice, poured a stiff shot of vodka into each, and topped them off with orange juice. Don came into the kitchen with a cheerful greeting.

"Hi, sweetheart. How was your—" He stopped cold as he saw Lilly standing at the counter, four partially empty pint bottles standing in a neat row.

"Here," she said, handing one of the glasses to Don. "We might as well have a drink while we talk about this." She went to the kitchen table, pulled out a chair and motioned to him. "Sit down."

They sat across the table, staring, each waiting for the other to break the silence. Don's mind was racing. Given time, he could have thought of a defense, some plausible explanation for all those bottles. But she'd caught him by surprise. At least she hadn't found all his hiding places.

"Well?" Lilly said. "What do you have to say? Is this the way you keep your promise?"

"Look, Lilly...I don't know what to say—"

"You need help, Don, professional help. You need to think about rehab."

"I don't know, Lilly. Old Mac could go ballistic on me. I could lose my job."

"You've always told me the company has a great health coverage. Jeezus, you've been there for eighteen years. How could rehab not be covered?"

"You don't get it. You come forward, admitting you have a problem, begging for help, it's a career killer."

"And the alternative? What are you going to do about this...this shitshow?" She motioned toward the bottles lined up on the counter.

"I don't know. I need some time to think. Just give me some time."

Lilly rose from the table, took her glass to the sink and poured the contents down the drain. She left Don sitting at the kitchen table. A moment later, the door to the bedroom slammed shut. Don shook his head, looked around, and downed his drink in three large gulps.

24

August 9, 2019

Crusty's Corner

One year ago, August 2018, a fifteen-year-old Swedish girl decided not to go to school. Instead, she took a large poster board and made a sign. It read *Skolstrejk for Klimatet* (School Strike for Climate). She took her sign to the front of the Swedish Parliament building and kept going back for about three weeks. And thus was born a movement, a children's crusade that hit a milestone on March 15 of this year when 1.6 million students, in cities all around the globe, walked out of class to observe *Skolstrejk for Klimatet.*

We have come to know the girl from Sweden. Her name is Greta Thunberg and she pursues her campaign for climate justice with a singular determination. Greta has been diagnosed with Asperger's Syndrome. She calls it her superpower, and she wields that power through words as sharp as her focus on the climate crisis.

"How dare you?" she demands of the United Nations Climate Action Summit.

"Did you hear what I just said? Is my microphone on?" she asks the Parliament of the U.K. Her questions were met with nervous laughter. Greta wasn't smiling.

It is said Greta Thunberg was inspired by the student survivors of mass murder at Marjory Stoneman Douglas High School in Parkland, Florida. The feeling runs both ways. Emma Gonzalez, one of the leaders of the Parkland students, is quoted as saying Greta's way of "inspiring steadfast students and shaming apathetic adults" has sparked a worldwide movement. Greta has twice been nominated for the Nobel Peace Prize.

And so, the little girl from Sweden calls out my generation again and again, pointing to the empirical evidence, citing the science, demanding that we take the hard steps required to meet the goals of the Paris Climate Accords.

One thing is clear: a new generation of leaders is coming. They know our failures and we will not be forgiven. They intend to remake the world. God bless them all.

—R.Q. Crutchfeld

25

The traffic on Highway 49 moved smoothly, heading south toward Auburn. Brett made a late start from Gold Ridge, but at the current pace, he'd be on time for his appointment with Dr. Bowman. He reached the section of the highway that became four-lane and, rather than speed up, the flow of vehicles ground to a halt.

Oh crap! He glanced at the clock on his dashboard. He hated being late. *Stay calm, Corcoran. If you're late, so be it. Bowman will understand.* The traffic inched forward. *Probably an accident up ahead. A wreck, or...* His heart began to race. He felt sweat dripping across his temples. *Just like a convoy. A goddamn convoy...* He looked ahead to the apron of the road. There was small cardboard box...

"IED! IED!" he screamed to warn the other drivers.

Oh my God. Oh shit. Stop it. You're in Auburn, not Mosul.

He leaned back in the seat and closed his eyes, trying to clear the scene that flooded his mind.

The driver behind him leaned on the horn.

Brett jolted upright. "You sonofabitch!" he shouted as he glared at the rearview mirror. "You goddamn sonofabitch!" He slammed the gearshift into Park, unlatched his seatbelt, threw the door open and jumped out of the car. "You got a problem, asshole? You want a piece of me? Well here I am! Bring it on!"

The driver of the car behind Brett was shocked, his eyes wide with fear. He raised his hands in surrender and mouthed the words, "I'm sorry, man..."

Cars in the adjacent lane began to move forward and Brett saw he was blocking his lane. He got back into his vehicle, fighting to control his rage, and pulled forward with the traffic.

In less than five minutes, he reached the intersection with Bell Road. Rather than turn right toward the VA office, he moved into the left turn lane. There was a McDonald's on the southeast corner. He pulled into the parking lot, went into the restaurant, and ordered a cup of coffee. He found an empty booth and sat down hard, his eyes fixed on the tabletop.

How could I do that? How could I lose control in the middle of Highway 49? Screaming at that guy like a crazy person... His heart raced again, his breath coming in gasps, as though he'd run a mile. He closed his eyes and counted backward from one hundred, trying to calm himself. *99 98 97 96 95...* This had worked in the past. It had to work now. *94 93 92 91...*

"Hey, mister!"

A small voice penetrated Brett's concentration. He opened his eyes. A boy no more than six-years-old stood next to his booth, looking up with large brown eyes.

"Here, mister." The boy placed a Happy Meal toy on the table, still in its plastic wrapper. "I hope you feel better." He turned and ran a dozen steps to where a young woman stood waiting. She clutched the boy's hand and they headed for the exit. The child looked over his shoulder and smiled.

Brett grabbed a napkin and clamped it over his eyes to hide the tears. Several minutes passed before he was able to call Dr. Bowman's office and tell the receptionist he could not keep his appointment. He finished his coffee and headed for his car in the parking lot, clutching the toy in his right hand.

26

A workout partner is a good thing, someone to get you off the couch when you'd rather watch SportsCenter, to push you forward when you'd rather not run another lap, or to snap, "Give me one more rep, come on, one more!" when you're tired of lifting. Brett and Joey D were good together, like ham and eggs. When Brett was slacking, Joey pushed, and vice versa. One plus one equaled more than two.

They used the high school field for batting practice, Brett throwing as Joey honed his swing, determined to take another shot at making the Gold Ridge Community College team. Brett would hit a little too, just to keep his hand in. Pitchers seldom bat at the college level, the designated hitter rule being in effect. Batting practice was Joey's thing, Brett's payback for Joey serving as his bullpen catcher.

On occasion, Webb Johnson would stop by to observe these sessions. He was no hitting coach, but like many old pitchers, he'd spent a lifetime analyzing hitters. He knew things. He knew Joey D had a beautiful left-handed stroke—no hitches, no obvious weak spots. And he knew one of the most important parts of a fine swing, the one that determined success or failure, was the space between the batter's ears. Tug McGraw's mantra applied directly to hitters: "Ya gotta believe!" Webb made it his job to make Joey DiFranco believe.

"Nice session, Joey. You're a pure hitter."

"Lookin' good, Joey D. We're gonna call you The Natural."

"Oh baby! That stroke is so sweet. Like honey on a Georgia peach."

One day Webb struck gold. "Joey D, I figured it out. I know who you remind me of."

"Yeah? Who's that, Webb?"

"Tony Gwynn. You're the Italian Tony Gwynn."

That brought roars of laughter from Joey and Brett, and Webb joined in the fun. But the seed was planted and the idea stuck. Joey never told anyone, but from that day forward he *was* Tony Gwynn. He took a Sharpie and wrote inside the bill of his cap: "What would Tony do?"

Joey DiFranco had the answer.

On a clear summer day, Brett and Joey tossed the ball back and forth, warming up for a hitting session. Brett made the familiar motion with his glove to indicate he was throwing a curve. The ball broke sharply, hit the heel of Joey's glove, and fell to the ground.

"Whoa! What was that?" Joey grinned. "Can you do that again?"

He tossed the ball to Brett who studied his grip, wound up and threw again; same sharp, late break, accompanied by a sizzling sound generated by the spin.

"What the hell! That's nasty!" Joey returned the ball and Brett did it again. "What are you doing?" Joey trotted to where Brett was standing.

"It's a 'spike curve'." Brett showed him the grip. "I watched an interview with Mike Mussina and he was showing how he threw it. Thought I'd give it a try. What do you think?"

"Are you kidding me? I can't wait to show this to Webb. He's gonna wet himself. I think you found your curve ball, buddy."

It was quiet at Foothill Batting Cages on a mid-week morning, except for the sound of a baseball slapping leather—the deep thud of a catcher's mitt, followed by the lighter pop of a fielder's glove. Brett began his bullpen session, Joey D in full catcher's gear, Webb manning the radar gun and the camcorder.

"Hey, Webb," Brett called. "Watch this."

"Heads up, Coach." Joey D smiled behind the catcher's mask. "You're gonna like this."

The pitch started waist high to a right-handed batter and broke sharply down and across the plate. Webb's eyes widened. Brett threw again, starting the ball higher, breaking it down into the strike zone. One more pitch, this time breaking low, as though targeting a left-handed hitter's back foot.

"Shee-it! Lookee here!" Webb stopped the camera and walked quickly to the mound. "Show me what you're doing, son."

Brett demonstrated the grip, his index finger raised like a knuckler, forcing the ball to spin off his middle finger. "I saw an interview with Mike Mussina. What do you think?"

The old man grinned ear to ear. "That's it, Brett. That's the breakin' pitch we've been looking for. And you did it all by yourself, didn't even need old Webb." He laughed out loud.

"It just feels right, Webb. I mean, I can spot it—start it high, low, in, out, bounce it in the dirt if I want. I don't know, it just feels good."

Joey D joined them on the mound where they stood smiling, talking about the breakthrough. In the middle of the good vibrations, Webb felt a sense of melancholy coming on. His teaching gig was coming to an end. Brett was well on his way to mastering the three tools—velocity, location, and movement. With this breakthrough, he now had four pitches to take into a game: four-seam fastball, two-seam fastball, changeup, and a sharp curve, all four with good movement. Brett was ready for the next step.

27

It was a sunny afternoon, temperature in the eighties, with a light breeze from the southwest. Webb, Brett, and Joey D sat in the third base dugout at Eagle's Stadium, waiting for Coach Harlon Millburn to arrive. Webb had arranged for Millburn to come and watch Brett work through a bullpen session. Fall practice for the community college team would begin in September and Webb was determined to showcase Brett's progress and dispel any lingering doubts Millburn may have.

Webb read a text message on his phone. "Millburn says he'll be 'bout thirty minutes late. Got held up in a faculty meeting. Says he'll text again when he's on his way."

"Should we start getting loose, Webb?" Brett sounded nervous, anxious to get started.

"Nah. Let's wait till we hear from him." Webb looked out at the diamond, admiring the work of the groundskeepers. The field had been well-tended during the offseason, the grass lush and green.

"Webb, what years did you play pro ball?" Joey D asked.

Webb laughed. "Interested in ancient history, eh?" He paused to jog his memory. "I signed with the Giants in 1958, right out of high school. I was in the organization for seven seasons, part of an eighth. Made it to Triple-A."

"No shit?" Joey grinned. "What then?"

"Had a real good year for the Tacoma Giants in '64. Pitched out of the bullpen mostly, but won five games as a starter, ERA under 3.00. I thought I'd get called up in September to close out the season."

"Yeah?"

"It didn't happen. Never got the call. Stung like a bitch. I would have been at Candlestick Park, in the same locker room with Willie Mays. Can you picture that? Mays, McCovey, Cepeda, Marichal, Perry, all those Hall of Fame guys."

"Wow! That would've been great. What came after that?"

"The usual sad story. Arm trouble, lots of pain, tried to pitch through it, made it worse. I got demoted all the way to Class-A Fresno by '66. Finally had to face the music and hang it up."

"But that's something, man. You were right there, one step away. That's way more than most guys ever get." Joey nudged the old man with his elbow and smiled.

Webb laughed. "Ah...it wasn't all bad. I was in love at the time, beautiful girl from Fresno. Man, oh man, she was a sweetheart. Smart as a whip, too."

Joey D and Brett turned to Webb. Was there more to the story?

"We had a little apartment, her and me, with a big tree right outside the bedroom window. We'd lay there, all cuddled up, and listen to the mourning doves. Those damn mourning doves goin' 'coo coo coo'." Webb paused, his eyes wet with memory. "To this day, every time I hear mourning doves, I think about that girl."

The dugout was still for a moment. Joey broke the silence.

"What happened to that girl, Webb?"

"Oh...she went to school back east, met her soulmate, started a family. We lost touch. I went to San Jose State, got my teaching credential, and wound up at Gold Ridge High." Webb laughed. "Wound up coachin' Brett's old man. 'Big Don' Corcoran. He was a pretty good thumber."

Webb's phone pinged and he looked at the screen. "Okay, Millburn's on his way. Should be here in about fifteen minutes. You guys start loosening up."

Brett and Joey D stepped out of the dugout and began to jog toward the centerfield flagpole, leaving Webb to think about mourning doves.

Harlon Millburn arrived with an air of irritation, as though this demand on his time was a pain in the ass. He'd agreed to watch Brett Corcoran work out but was surprised to see Joey DiFranco there as well. *I cut both of these guys last year, for God's sake. What the hell am I doing here?*

Brett was warmed up and ready to go. He went to the mound and Joey D took his place behind the plate in full catcher's gear. Brett made a half-dozen pitches, working up to full speed, while Millburn and Webb went behind the backstop with their radar guns. The two coaches timed a couple of pitches and found their guns were in sync. Webb gave the thumbs up to Brett and the session turned serious.

The first two fastballs Brett threw hit ninety-five miles per hour and caught Millburn's attention. Webb signaled for a changeup and Brett executed perfectly; eighty-six MPH with nice movement. He threw another changeup for good measure; same result. Webb signaled for the curve, and it broke sharply. Joey D almost missed it.

Millburn was focused now. "Throw the curve again, Corcoran," he called out. Maybe it had been a fluke.

Brett started the next pitch about thigh high and it dove into the dirt behind the plate, the kind of curve that gets a swing-through from a hitter. Joey D blocked it nicely, like a good catcher should.

The workout continued, Brett showing four competitive pitches. The two coaches moved out to the field, behind the mound, Webb calling out the spots for Brett to hit. The young man's command was impressive. The session ended with a four-seam fastball that hit ninety-six on the gun. Brett and Joey D went to the dugout to towel off, leaving Webb and Millburn to chat.

"Well?" Webb grinned at the skipper. "Whataya think?"

Millburn made an attempt at disinterest but failed. He decided to play it straight. "I gotta say that's the best I've seen in quite a while. That damn curveball is electric. You teach him that?"

"Nope. Can't take credit for that one. The kid picked it up himself."

"Well…" Millburn scuffed the ground with his toe. "He looks good, but it depends on what he shows when there is a hitter up there with a whupin' stick."

The two men walked to the dugout where Brett and Joey D were cooling down.

Millburn smiled. "Very impressive, Brett. You've come a long way since last October. What are your plans, son?"

"Joey and I are enrolled and registered for classes, Coach. We want to come out for fall ball and make the team. Joey D's made some big moves, too. I've been throwing batting practice for him. He can really rake."

It dawned on Harlon Millburn that these two young men were presenting as a tandem. *You take the big strong blonde, you get the short dark one, too.* He didn't like having his arm twisted, but the numbers on the radar gun and the pop of the catcher's mitt were still fresh in his mind.

Brett continued to twist. "Joey D's a natural in the outfield, but you just saw him behind the plate. He's become a fine receiver. I'm thinking you could use a guy like that."

Millburn was impressed. This Corcoran kid had grown a pair. "Tell you what, fellas. I'd love to see both of you turn out for fall ball. I can't make any promises, but I like what you showed me today. Both of youse."

There were smiles all around. It was a step forward, but there were many more ahead.

28

September 30, 2019

Crusty's Corner

By now we've all read the transcript (or was it a summary?) of the July 25, 2019, phone call between President Donald Trump and President Volodymyr Zelensky of Ukraine. The President tells us the call was "perfect." There was no *quid pro quo*. Nothing to see here, folks. It's all deep state fake news.

I wonder if the President is reading the same document his administration released to the press? Sure sounds like a *quid pro quo* to me. *You want that $400 million aid package, Mr. Z., you're going to have to gin up investigations into the Bidens and that nefarious company called Burisma.*

Here's another fun fact: the call took place the day after Robert Mueller testified before the House Intelligence Committee. Not the resolute, vigorous, unshakable Mueller we were expecting, but a diminished, even frail Mueller, saying, *It's all in the report, folks. Do with it what you will.*

Suddenly the playing field has been tilted and a whole bunch of Democrats are in favor of an impeachment inquiry. Until now, Speaker Nancy Pelosi has been firm in her belief that impeachment should only be considered if there is bipartisan support. Let's face it, there is none.

Republicans in the House of Representatives, and especially in the Senate, are steadfast with Trump. If the President is impeached, he will be acquitted. And then what?

Nancy Pelosi had it right: impeachment requires bipartisan support. But the Speaker of the House serves at the pleasure of her caucus and one thing Speaker Pelosi knows how to do is count.

Buckle up, folks. It's going to be a turbulent winter.

—R.Q. Crutchfeld

29

There are occasions when a party breaks out on its own—no planning, no notification, just an organic happening. Suddenly there's a crowd and there's music and laughter and everyone is holding a drink and the party is on. It may begin in one location, then migrate to another. Word gets out, the crowd grows, and sometimes things get out of hand. Or not. It depends on your point of view, whether or not you are a member of the party.

That was the situation on a fall evening at the Hotel Truro. A group of men and women gathered in the hotel lounge to celebrate something—no one could remember exactly what—and a party erupted. It migrated upstairs to Suite 315. Bottles of liquor appeared along with ice in a large plastic bucket and various mixes in liter bottles. Jack and Coke was the popular choice, followed closely by Margaritas. The Margarita crowd devolved into tequila shots and things got interesting. Country music blared on the radio, bursts of laughter rocked the room, and folks in neighboring rooms began to call the front desk to complain.

The hotel management sent a staff member to Suite 315 with a polite but firm request to keep it down. And so, the party began to break up, all but the die-hards calling it a night and heading for home. Don Corcoran was one of the die-hards.

Across town, Brett Corcoran was busy making a peanut butter and jelly sandwich. Ramona was working late at Rosalita's and Brett had the apartment to himself. He was opening a bag of chips when the phone rang.

"Hello?"

"Hi, is this Brett? Brett Corcoran?" The woman on the phone sounded cheerful.

"Yeah. Who's calling?"

"You don't know me, but I'm a friend of your dad's." There was noise in the background, muffled laughter. "Listen, we kinda had a party after work today, a little celebration. Anyway, its breaking up and I think you should come and get Don. He's in no shape to drive."

Brett cringed. *Oh shit. Here we go.* "Where are you?"

"What? I couldn't hear you." The background noise swelled. "Hey, keep it down! Sorry…what did you say?"

"Where are you calling from?"

"Oh. It's the Hotel Truro, Suite 315."

"Okay. I'll be there in about fifteen minutes."

Brett slipped on his shoes, found his keys and headed for the door. Maybe it was good the woman called him rather than Lilly. Or not. *Ah hell, it's no secret. The old man's got a problem.* Brett hurried to his car and headed into town.

Brett knocked on the door marked 315, waited a moment, and knocked again. The door opened and an attractive woman with flaming red hair stared at him. She looked to be mid-thirties, wearing a green dress that matched her eyes. The eyes were a little bloodshot.

"Hi! Are you Brett?" Her smile revealed gleaming white teeth.

"Yes. Are you the one I spoke to on the phone?" The room was empty but for the pretty redhead.

"Yeah. Come on in. Don's in the bathroom. He should be out in a minute."

Brett could hear singing coming from behind a closed door across the room, someone trying to belt out "Okie from Muskogee." The door opened and Don Corcoran stumbled out, his tie hanging loose, shirt collar unbuttoned.

"Brett! Hey, buddy, what are you doin' here? Hey, did you meet my friend? What's your name, honey?"

The woman's pretty face pinched in anger. Her voice dripped sarcasm. "It's Seeya…as in See-ya later, pal. Brett here is gonna take you home."

"Yeah, come on, dad. Do you have everything? Give me your keys. We'll get your car later."

Don shuffled his feet. His expression changed and his voice took on a low, dull tone. "Oh…I done a bad thing…I done another bad thing…Now George ain't gonna let me tend them rabbits."

"What the hell's he talking about? What rabbits?" The woman gave Brett a puzzled look.

"He's trying to quote Steinbeck. Doing a damn poor job of it. Come on, Dad, let's go. The party's over."

Don took up the theme, singing, "Turn out the lights / The party's over…"

Brett took his arm and led him out of the room.

Lilly answered her cell phone on the third ring. "Hi, Brett. What's going on?"

"Are you at home, Lilly?"

"Yeah, I had to work late. Just got here. The place is dark. Do you know where your dad is?"

"He's here with me, sound asleep on the couch. There was some kind of celebration after work and he got a snoot full."

"Oh geez. Did he get in any trouble?"

Brett flashed on his father's riff on *Of Mice and Men.* "No, he didn't do anything bad. Just too much booze. I brought him here because it's closer. He's out cold, snoring like a buzz saw."

"You want me to come get him?"

"No, that's okay. Ramona's working late at Rosalita's. Let him sleep it off. I'll get him home in the morning."

"God, Brett, what am I gonna do? I can't convince him to get help. I've tried everything, threatened to leave, threatened to flush his car keys down the toilet. He won't listen."

Brett's heart went out to this woman he once hated. "I've tried too, Lilly. Won't listen to me either. Maybe as a group—" He pictured himself, Lilly, Webb, Ramona, surrounding his father, attempting to intervene in this slow-motion train wreck. He left the sentence unfinished.

They made plans for the morning, getting Don home, recovering his car, and closed with a promise to make a bigger, more desperate plan, before it was too late.

⌒⫞⌒

Brett tried to get comfortable in the overstuffed chair next to the couch. He didn't want Ramona to walk in from work and find his father there without explanation. *Maybe I should have taken him out to the house. Nah, damn winding roads, and it's too far out. Better here. Ramona will understand. Geez, what if tonight is the night her roommate decides to come here instead of her boyfriend's place? How embarrassing would that be? Okay, so if it happens you'll deal with it...*

Brett wasn't sure how long he'd been asleep when he heard his father stumbling around the room. His eyes snapped open, he reached for the lamp next to the chair and fumbled for the switch.

Don bumped into the coffee table in the dark. "Joanne? Joanne? Where are we? Joanne?"

The light came on and Brett was on his feet. "Dad, it's okay. It's okay. I'm here."

His father squinted in the sudden light. "Brett, is that you? Where's Mom? Where are we?"

"It's okay, Dad. We're at Ramona's place. You're okay."

Don looked around, coming back to reality. "Where's the bathroom, Brett. I need the bathroom."

Brett took his father's arm and led him down the short hall to the bathroom. Don entered and closed the door. Brett went back to the living room to wait. *God, what a night. He's stumbling around, calling Mom's name. Got to get him help while he has brain cells left alive.* He checked the clock: nearly eleven. *Ramona should be leaving work soon. I'd better text her so she knows what to expect. Damn, why didn't I think of that before.*

30

It takes all kinds, or so they say, and Gold Ridge was no exception. As Hud Bannon put it, "You start separating the saints from the sinners, you're lucky to end up with Abraham Lincoln." From the Bitter Creek flophouse on the edge of town to the executive offices of The Sherman Group, from the campus of the community college to Crusty's Corner, you'd find the good, the bad, and the undecided. And it was so among Miss Margret's art students at the Uptown Gallery.

Ramona was engaged in a modeling session at the gallery, upstairs in the large open room, a dozen students sketching away at their easels. Brett took the stairs two at a time and waited in the back of the room, mulling over where to take his lady love for a sandwich when the class ended. He was amazed once again at how comfortable Ramona was posing in the nude—relaxed, natural, and very beautiful.

Brett noticed one of the students fumbling with something in his lap. The man lifted the object—an iPhone—aimed it at Ramona and pressed the white button at the bottom of the screen. Brett walked to where the man was sitting and placed a heavy hand on his shoulder.

"What are you doing?" Brett said quietly.

"What? Nothing. What's it to you?" He jerked the phone out of sight and attempted to stuff it in his pocket.

"Give me the phone…now." Brett's voice was firm.

The man was short and heavy set, thin brown hair covering a bald spot, thick horn-rimmed glasses obscuring his dark eyes.

"I'm not giving you my phone. Who the hell are you?"

"I'm the guy who's gonna kick your ass, right here in front of the class, if you don't give me the phone." Brett waited. "Hand it over or I'll break your arm taking it away."

A second later, the phone was in Brett's hand. Several students had turned to witness the exchange and the instructor came quickly to where Brett was standing.

"Brett, what's going on? Is there a problem?" Margret's face drained of color.

"Hi, Margret. No, there's no problem—now. We can talk after class."

⌇⌇⌇

The grandfather clock struck the hour and the room emptied quickly, the other students aware a situation was coming to a boil. Ramona put on her robe and went behind the screen at the side of the room to dress.

Margret, the instructor, motioned for Brett and the man named Ralph to join her.

"Okay, you two, what's going on." She looked from one to the other.

Ralph spoke first. "This guy forced me to give him my phone. I want it back. Now!"

"He was snapping pictures of Ramona. God knows what he planned to do with them. He's not getting his phone back until every shot is deleted."

"Ralph, is that true? You know that's a violation of our policy. You can't take pictures of the models." Margret's face was drawn in anger.

"Oh, big deal! She's up there naked for all the world to see. What does she care?"

"It's not for 'all the world,' Ralph. You know that. She is posing for you as a serious art student."

Brett lifted the phone. "I want your password so I can delete the photos."

"I'm not giving you my damn password." Ralph stood his ground.

"Suit yourself, Ralph. I'm gonna take a hammer and beat this thing to a thousand pieces."

Ramona joined the group. "Hey. What's going on?"

Ralph looked at Ramona, then at Brett and Margret. His face turning beet red. He grabbed his portfolio and ran for the door.

Margret shook her head. "Sorry, Brett. I'll make sure it doesn't happen again.'

Brett took Ramona's arm. "Come on, babe. I'll fill you in." He dropped the offending phone in his pocket as they left the room.

Burger Haven, their favorite shop for burgers and fries, was just down the street from the Uptown Gallery. Brett and Ramona took their trays to a booth by the window and dug in, the juicy burgers dripping on the wide white platters. Their discussion continued between bites.

"Look, Ramona, I think you should quit your modeling job. There's too many creeps out there just showing up for a peep show."

"But the money really helps, Brett. I've got tuition, fees, books, uniforms. It adds up fast."

"I know, but we're sharing expenses now. I don't make much at Big 5, but I can help out more. Do you really need the modeling money?"

"I just hate letting one little pervert run me out of a perfectly legitimate job."

"There's no telling what he had planned for the pictures, Ramona. What if he dumped 'em out on the Internet?"

"Yeah…not good."

"What if he did that and your parents saw it? What would they think?"

A pained expression crossed Ramona's face. She didn't reply.

Brett had a sudden thought. He pulled Ralph's phone from his pocket and tried a password: R-A-L-P-H. The screen lit up with an array of icons.

"Wow. That was easy. Let's see what old Ralph has stored here."

He pressed the Photo icon and began to scroll. There were a dozen photos with the current date, depicting Ramona in several poses. He scrolled further and found more from an earlier session. He started over and began deleting all he could find, his burger growing colder by the minute.

"Geez, this guy is unbelievable. I'm definitely gonna take a hammer to this damn phone."

Ramona swallowed hard. "Okay, I'll call Margret and cancel my sessions. My figure modeling career is over."

Brett was no techie, but he knew enough to know Ralph could have sent the pictures anywhere, or stored them in the cloud, or God only knows what else. The possibilities made him shudder.

31

The baseball stadium at Gold Ridge Community College was known as The Nest, short for Eagle's Nest, its official title. The grandstand was an impressive structure for a small school, capable of seating five hundred fans, constructed of steel and concrete and faced with locally quarried stone. The outfield fence—well-built chain link, eight feet high, covered in dark green canvas—defined a symmetric playing field, three hundred and ten feet down the foul lines, three seventy in the power alleys, and four hundred to straight-away center. It was a fine facility in every way, the result of a community fund-raising effort. Now a second drive was underway to add lights.

Beyond the right field fence was a second diamond with no grandstand or fencing, other than the backstop. The outfield ended where the pine forest began. The field was playable, the result of concerted effort by the groundskeeping crew, but in no way could it compare to The Nest. A small metal sign affixed to the backstop read, simply, "Field II."

During the fall practice season, when the number of players trying to make the team ranged between thirty-five and forty, the coaching staff ran intra-squad games on both fields. The highly valued players and presumed starters were assigned to The Nest, while the rest made their way to Field II, known as The Duce. If one were assigned to The Nest, the goal was to stay there at all costs. On the other hand, if assigned to The Duce, one fought fiercely to move up.

The sun was setting on a mild October evening as the coaching staff assembled in Harlon Millburn's office. The group consisted of Millburn's three paid assistants, plus four volunteers from the community who turned out for love of the game. The task at hand was to assess the week of fall practice just completed.

The discussion centered around the group assigned to The Nest: who was hot, who was not, were there any injuries, any bad actors whose attitudes may need adjustment?

Coach Millburn looked at his watch, ready to wrap up the meeting. "Okay, what's up on The Duce? Anybody there we need to think about moving up?"

Two coaches spoke at once: "Yeah, I got one for you!"

"Whoa," Millburn said. "One at a time. Marty, you go first."

"It's this kid Joey DiFranco. He's been ripping the cover off the ball. Seems like every ball he hits is a line drive. And he's solid behind the plate, too."

"And?" Millburn looked skeptical.

"And I think he moves up. Let's see what he can do against our best."

Millburn turned to the other assistant. "And what have you got, Jerry?"

"Brett Corcoran, Coach. He's been lights out. Definitely the best stuff of any pitcher on The Duce."

Millburn frowned. "You know, we cut both of these guys last October. What changed?"

"I suspect good old fashion hard work," Marty said. "Joey D got a lot stronger, that's clear. And he's squaring up every good pitch he sees."

"Same with Corcoran," Jerry added. "Hard work, I mean. He's been training with a guy named Webb Johnson who played some pro ball, coached at the high school back in the day."

Millburn checked his watch again. "I'm inclined to keep 'em where they are for now. Let's see how committed they are."

"Big mistake," said Jerry. "No offense, Coach. They've proved their commitment and it shows. I say bring 'em up."

Millburn looked from one coach to the other. Both held eye contact. "Okay. You got it. Move 'em to The Nest. I hope you two aren't wasting my time." He looked around the room. "See you guys on Monday."

Brett entered the locker room Monday afternoon, the place loud with the usual jock talk. Joey D was there already, scanning the assignment list posted on a bulletin board. Brett saw him clench his fist and shout, "Yes!"

"Hey, Joey D, what's up, man?"

"We're moved up, Brett. Both of us. We're on The Nest today. You're pitching a couple of innings and I'm starting in center, then moving behind the plate when you come in." Joey D grinned from ear to ear. He held up his right hand and Brett slapped a high-five.

Jerry, the assistant coach, came from behind and grabbed them by the shoulders. "Way to go, guys. Now don't make me look bad." He smiled and walked away.

Brett felt the butterflies take flight in his stomach. "Okay, buddy, we're gonna get our shot. And there's no going back. We're done with The Duce." He threw his arm around Joey's shoulder as they walked toward their lockers.

Webb had advised Don Corcoran that his teaching sessions with Brett were done for the time being. No need for Don to keep writing checks. But Webb wasn't one to leave things to chance. He went to the public library, logged on to the Internet and found a few of his peers were still active in the scouting ranks. After several calls, he reached a former teammate.

"Hello?"

"Yeah, may I speak to Curley Grimble?"

"Who's calling?" The deep, raspy voice was familiar.

"Curley, is that you? It's Webb Johnson."

"What? You're kiddin' me? Webb Johnson, my old roomie?"

"Hey, they always had us black guys room together. Am I right?"

"Damn, Webb! I thought you was dead. How the hell are ya?"

The two old teammates shared a laugh and caught up quickly.

Charles "Curley" Grimble was a scout for the Colorado Rockies, assigned to cover Northern California and Nevada from his base in the San Francisco area. They shared a few war stories, then Webb got down to business.

"Curley, I've got a kid I've been workin' with. I think it would be worth your while to take a look."

"Okay, Webb, I'm listening."

Webb provided a quick rundown on Brett Corcoran. Big, strong, hard-throwing, making great strides with a changeup and a sharp curve, fastball sits in the mid-nineties.

Grimble's interest was stirred. "How old is this boy?"

"Just turned twenty-three."

"Whoa...that's a little long in the tooth. Has he ever been drafted?"

"No. He's been out of the game. Served nearly four years in the Army. Two tours in Iraq."

"Damn, Webb. I don't know. Let's say we like him. By the time he comes through our minor league system, he'll be what—twenty-six, twenty-seven? That's a stretch."

"You're lookin' at it wrong, Curley."

"How so?"

"While all your other hot prospects were throwin' their little hearts out, rackin' up innings and pitch counts, blowin' out their arms and gettin' Tommy John surgery, Corcoran didn't touch a baseball. He got bigger, stronger, grew into his body. And he's low mileage, Curley. All those innings and all those pitches are still in the tank."

Grimble laughed at Webb's analysis. "Okay, buddy, ya got me. I'll take a look."

"We can save you some driving time, too. The Eagles are coming down to Sacramento to scrimmage against Sac City College. The way things are going, you'll be able to see him pitch then."

They agreed to stay in touch and work out the details, then reminisced a while longer before ending the call. Webb checked the list on his note pad. He had a few more calls to make.

32

October 31, 2019

Crusty's Corner

The World Series ended last night with the Washington Nationals defeating the Houston Astro 6 - 2 to claim the trophy for the first time in franchise history. It's always fun when the series goes to Game 7. After 162 regular season games and multiple playoff rounds, it all came down to one game. For a baseball fan, the anticipation was terrific, and the game did not disappoint.

Nats pitcher Stephen Strasberg was named the MVP, and rightfully so. And the series provided a showcase for many of the brightest young stars of the game. But for this old newsboy, the most satisfying outcome was to see two battle scarred veterans earn World Series rings. I'm talking about Howie Kendrick and Ryan Zimmerman.

Howie was a favorite of mine when he played for the L.A. Angels, always solid, reliable, and productive, if unspectacular. To see him contribute big hits throughout the postseason brought a smile to my face. His homerun last night gave the Nats a lead they would not relinquish.

In 2005, Ryan Zimmerman became the first draft pick of the newly relocated Washington franchise. His career has been plagued by injury, but he always found a way to bounce back.

Case in point: Zimmerman began the 2017 season with a hot streak. Through 32 games, he was hitting .410 with 12 homeruns. He went on to an outstanding season, including a start at first base in the All Star Game and recognition as Comeback Player of the Year.

Here's an interesting statistic: Walk-off Homeruns. Jim Thome holds the all-time record with 13. There are six guys tied at 12 (Babe Ruth, Jimmy Foxx, Stan Musial, Mickey Mantle, Frank Robinson, and Albert Pujols). And then three players tied with 11 (Tony Perez, David Ortiz, and Ryan Zimmerman). Yep, there's that name again, and that is one hell of list to be on.

The great ones don't play the game with the goal of winding up on some obscure list. They play to be known as champions, to be on the field celebrating when the last out of the final game of the season is made. It felt right that Howie and Zimm got to celebrate last night at Minute Maid Park in Houston.

—R.Q. Crutchfeld

33

The small shop situated on Main Street presented a friendly face to passersby. The brick façade was painted bright white, the door and window framing a high-gloss black. The display window featured poster boards with photos of homes for sale and apartments for rent. The message was clear: Come on in, we're here to help.

Brett pushed the door open and stepped inside. The bell on the doorjamb announced his presence. A man emerged from a back room with a broad smile and an outstretched hand.

"Hello! Welcome to Bennett Realty. How can I help you?"

The man appeared to be in his fifties, medium height and build, dressed in slacks, a white dress shirt and tie.

"Hi, I'm looking for Roy Bennett. We have an appointment." Brett shook hands and returned the smile.

"Well, you came to the right place. I'm Roy Bennett. And you must be Brett Corcoran. Pleasure to meet you. Your dad and I are old friends."

"Nice to meet you, Mr. Bennett. My dad says you're the man to see about rentals. Like I said on the phone, I have a friend who's looking for an apartment. He should be here any minute now. He's always on time."

Bennett pulled an index card out of the breast pocket of his shirt. "Let me check my notes…seventy-nine-year-old man, single, looking for a one-bedroom apartment, preferably ground floor. I take it he's spry, still pretty active?"

"Oh yeah, he's active all right." Brett laughed. He hadn't expected that question in reference to Webb Johnson.

"Good. I've got a couple of places to show you. Relatively new buildings, modern amenities. There's not a lot of inventory around town, but both of these are quality locations." He paused and looked toward the front window. "Whoa. Look at this."

Brett turned toward the window where an elderly black man was scanning the photos in the window display. "Oh, here's my friend now." He glanced at his watch. "Right on time, too." Webb opened the front door and walked into the shop. Brett introduced him. "Roy Bennett, this is Webb Johnson. Webb, meet Roy Bennett. He's going to help us today."

Bennett hesitated, then offered his hand. "Mr. Johnson. Nice to meet you." His eyes darted between Brett and Webb.

"My pleasure. And please call me Webb. I hear you have some places to show me."

"Yeah. Right. Okay…before we head out, let me make a couple of quick calls to let them know we're coming. Make yourselves comfortable. Would you like some coffee? No? Okay, I'll be right back." Bennett disappeared into the back room.

Webb looked at Brett. "Oh shit! You didn't tell him. Am I right?"

"Tell him what?"

"That I'm black."

"No. It didn't come up. I mean, why would it matter…?" Brett's voice trailed away. Of course, it mattered. Of course, he should have mentioned it. Now he'd set Webb up to be embarrassed. He felt a tightness in his throat. Blood rushed to his cheeks.

Bennett came out of the back room, a silly look on his face. "Jeez, guys, I'm afraid I have some bad news. Both of the places I had lined up to show you have been rented. I'm afraid I've got nothing for you today. I apologize, seriously. Maybe we can reschedule?"

Brett's temples throbbed. He could barely hear the conversation that followed. In less than a minute, he and Webb were standing on the sidewalk in front of Bennett Realty. Brett's anger was boiling.

"Okay, Brett, take a deep breath. Bring it down, son. It's okay. This is not my first rodeo. I'm seventy-nine freakin' years old and I've dealt with it my whole life. I'll be fine. Are you listening to me?"

"Holy crap, Webb! I'm so sorry. I'd like to slap the silly grin off Bennett's smug-ass face."

"Deep breath, son. Breathe in, breathe out. I know your temper and I know how hard you're workin' with that doc at the VA. Don't let this blow up your progress. Let's just move on."

"But I really want to see you get out of the Bitter Creek Hotel, Webb. You can afford it, and that place isn't for you anymore. I'm really sorry. I screwed this up big time."

"Hey, I'll find a place. It'll just take some time. Look, I'm gonna head for home. We've got a bullpen session scheduled for tomorrow. I'll see you then. Okay?" Webb reached out to rub Brett's arm. He smiled and walked away.

Brett turned and looked through the window into the shop where Bennett sat at a small desk, his head down, hard at work on something. Brett went to the door and stepped inside. Bennett looked up, surprised.

"So, both places were suddenly rented. Seems odd, don't you think?"

"Now look, Corcoran, you could've let me know. At least then I'd have known where to look for vacancies."

"Oh really? Are there lines on your little map, places a black man can't live? You realize this is 2020, not 1963, right?"

"Come on. I don't make the rules in this town. I just have to live by 'em."

"You know what…I served in Iraq with black, brown, every color of the rainbow, and we all bled the same bright red for this country. Honor, duty, the American way. And for what? So we can come home and play by your rules?" Brett placed his hands on the desk and leaned in.

Bennett rolled his chair back, glancing left and right. "Okay now, wait just a minute—"

Brett laughed. "Don't worry, Mr. Bennett. I'm feeling pretty steady today. You're getting off easy. You get to keep all your teeth."

He turned and left the shop. The door slammed behind him.

34

Psychologists have studied motivation for decades, and yet, the answers are still open to debate. We look to Mazlow and his Hierarchy of Needs, or Herzberg and his Hygiene vs. Motivator theory. These and many other theories make sense—to academics. But what if you are a man headed for rock bottom, lucky to have avoided catastrophe so far, deep in denial that anything is wrong? What will cause that man to change behavior?

For Don Corcoran, the motivator was fear. He scared the shit out of himself. He got drunk to the point of unconsciousness, woke up dazed and confused in a strange dark place, calling out for a wife dead more than four years. He didn't need an intervention by his loved ones to tell him it was time to change. The specter of the dark place hung over him like a black cloud.

The old Methodist Church on Second Street was a classic of its era, a red brick structure that included an impressive bell tower. The current building opened in the 1920s, replacing the original wooden sanctuary that had been destroyed by fire. The chapel contained solid oak pews that could seat two hundred souls, and the north and south walls were lined with beautiful stained-glass windows. The basement level served as a social hall and included a kitchen and a few classrooms for Sunday School. There, in one of the Sunday School rooms, a local chapter of Alcoholics Anonymous held its meetings.

Folding chairs were arranged in a circle to accommodate as many as twenty. On this night in early November, about fifteen people had gathered. Most were men in their forties and fifties, though a handful of women had turned out. The racial mix reflected Gold Ridge itself—predominantly white with a few black and brown faces. They clustered in small groups, talking, laughing, renewing acquaintances.

An elderly black man entered the room, his hand placed firmly on the back of a tall blue-eyed man. He guided his friend to a seat in the circle as the meeting was about to begin.

A stack of manila folders and books sat on a chair reserved for the group leader. A slender man with black hair and piercing gray eyes came to the chair and set the materials on the floor.

"Okay, folks, let's get started." He waited for the people milling about to take a seat in the circle. "I'm Carl and I'm your leader for tonight. Let's all join hands…and join me in the Serenity Prayer."

> *God, grant me the serenity to accept the things I cannot change, courage to change the things I can, and wisdom to know the difference.*

"Amen. Now, you know we're pretty informal here," Carl continued. "We keep it simple. We'll go around the circle and invite each of you to give his or her testimony." He turned to the woman seated to his right. "Would you start us off this evening?"

The woman smiled and looked around the circle. "Hi! I'm Sue and I'm an alcoholic."

The room erupted, "Hi, Sue!"

"I've been sober ten months and two days…" She paused and looked down. "And every damn day is a struggle. There isn't a day goes by that I don't think about taking a drink. But I've been down that shithole and I'm not going back." Sue continued, describing a ruined career, a wrecked marriage, relationships with her children strained to the breaking point. She concluded, "…and so I get down on my knees every morning and ask God to help me make it through the day. And for ten months and two days, the answer has been *Yes*."

All around the circle there were cries of *Amen* and *You go girl* and *Praise God*.

Sue passed the baton to a guy named Derek and the testimony continued, each person with a story to tell of havoc and violence to their lives.

Don felt the hot breath of terror on his neck as his turn to speak neared. What would he say? What was he ready to *own*? Could he still sprint for the door and get the hell out of there?

Jeezus, think dummy, think! What am I gonna say? I'll make something up, something convincing. Listen to these stories. God, what am I doing here? I'm not gonna talk about the accident. Not gonna talk about Joanne. They have no right to know about that. I don't know these people from Adam. I'm not opening my life to strangers. They're not gonna hear how I killed my wife…how the accident happened, the car, the road, the tree. No way in hell!

And then it was Don's turn.

He looked around the room, locked eyes with the leader, tears streaming down his face, his voice barely a croak. "I'm Don," he said, "and I'm an alcoholic…" He felt Webb's arm around his shoulder, felt a squeeze from the strong old hand.

It was a start.

35

Sacramento City College boasts a long and storied baseball program that has produced many major league players, including Larry Bowa, Buck Martinez, Greg Vaughn, Fernando Vina, and Chris Bosio. The Panthers own five state championship trophies and are perennial contenders to represent Northern California in the State tournament played in Fresno every Memorial Day weekend. In contrast, Gold Ridge Community College was a relative upstart, a small school from the foothills trying to compete with the big boys.

Union Stadium sits like a jewel in the heart of the Sac City campus. The Gold Ridge Eagles, clad in their spotless traveling uniforms, stepped onto the manicured green diamond with more than a little trepidation. The public address system boomed rock anthems to entertain the pregame crowd.

The section of the grandstand behind home plate began to fill with scouts, men both young and old, each carrying a small case that held a radar gun. They brought small folios with all the necessary forms and materials to record their observations, information that would be fed to cross-checkers and player development personnel higher up in their organizations. Several major league teams were represented, plus a handful of universities. They were there to watch a fall scrimmage simply because it was what they did.

Webb Johnson and Curley Grimble found seats in the second row, a little toward the first base side, with good sight lines to see and chart pitches. Curley, a charter member of the Good Old Boys Club, called hello and exchanged comments with the men around him. All the usual suspects were there. Webb was quiet, drawn into himself, his stomach a little jumpy with anticipation. This would be a serious test for his pupil, Brett Corcoran.

The game started on schedule and Joey D stepped in as the leadoff hitter for the Eagles. He lined the second pitch into right field for a single. Webb smiled and clapped his hands. *Stay hot, Joey D.* But the Eagles followed with three weak outs and the Panthers came to bat.

Sac City's lineup was big and strong and they proceeded to tee off on the Eagles' starting pitcher, scoring two runs on three hits in the bottom of the first. That set the pattern for the game—the Panthers flexing their muscles, the Eagles fighting to keep the game within reach.

Brett was scheduled to pitch the fourth, fifth, and sixth innings and the score was 6 – 0 when he trotted to the mound. Webb tried to calm his nerves. He could imagine what Brett was feeling. Many of the scouts had packed it in and drifted away. They were there to see specific players and after three innings, it was time to hit the road. It was only fall ball.

The lineup had turned over and the top of the Panthers' order would come to bat. Brett jumped ahead with a good fastball, followed by a nice changeup. On his third pitch, the hitter sent a ground ball through the hole between short and third for a base hit. Brett walked the next batter on five pitches and found himself in a jam. A sharp curve and a fastball on the inside corner put him ahead of the number three hitter. A changeup resulted in a grounder to short that turned into a 6-4-3 double play, the runner from second advancing to third. Now Brett faced the Panthers' clean-up hitter, Josh Kilkenny, one of the best in the league. Kilkenny had a homerun earlier in the game.

Brett and Joey D had discussed Kilkenny, a powerful right-handed hitter. The word was he had one hole in his swing: he did not like the ball up and in. Brett's first pitch was a four-seamer attacking the alleged hole. Strike one. The next pitch was a sharp curve that broke over the outside corner. Strike two. Kilkenny had taken both pitches, doing his best "Casey at the Bat" impression. Brett threw a changeup just off the outside corner at the knees. Kilkenny wasn't biting. Ball one. It was time to go back inside. Brett fired a four-seamer up under Kilkenny's hands. Kilkenny swung and missed. Strike three.

Brett and Joey D trotted for the dugout while the scouts scribbled on their note cards. *Who the hell is this Corcoran? Have you got book on him? Not me, I got nothin'. I had 96 mph on that last pitch.*

Curley Grimble smiled at his old friend, Webb Johnson. "Well, I'll be damned. The kid's got some serious stuff."

Brett sent the Panthers' down 1-2-3 in the fifth and sixth innings, striking out three hitters along the way. Eagles coach Harlon Millburn was impressed. So were the few scouts who stuck around for the later innings.

For Curley Grimble, it was an entirely different feeling. He was falling in love.

Curley led Webb to his SUV in the parking lot behind the left field fence at Union Stadium. He unlocked the tailgate and lifted it so they could sit and talk.

"I really like him, Webb. I mean what's not to like? He's big, strong, got a good frame, and his stuff is just nasty. There's a lot to build on. I'm sure he could add another pitch, maybe a slider..." Curley trailed off.

"And? Sounds like you got more to say."

"He needs experience, some games under his belt. I mean there's literally nothing since he left high school. The kid needs at least one solid season—maybe two—before I could even think about putting him on our board for the draft."

"Yeah, okay. I hear ya." Webb nodded.

"You know, it would be better for Brett if he was in one of the stronger programs. One like Sac City. I'm thinking of a potential draft slot. From a small school like Gold Ridge, he's probably going to go in a lower round of the draft. There won't be much signing money. With a stronger program, more exposure…who knows."

"I know you're right, Curley, but he'll never leave Gold Ridge."

"Why's that?"

"He's in love. His lady is there. She's a nursing student."

"So, he'd give it all up for love, Webb?"

"Hey, you haven't met this girl. She is a *person*, Curley. Know what I mean? A real, honest to God person. If you met her, talked to her for five minutes, you'd understand."

The old teammates chatted a while longer, letting the cars empty out of the parking lot. It was clear: the ball was in Brett Corcoran's hands.

36

November 20, 2019

Crusty's Corner

One of the interesting items to come out of the Impeachment Hearings is the fact that the name of the Ukrainian capital has changed. For as long as I can remember, it was known as Kiev (Kee-ev). Now, as a result of the hearings, we have learned to say Kyiv (Keev). Turns out the Ukrainians made this official way back in 1995. Who knew?

Ambassador Gordon Sondland testified today. Committee members delved into his famous visit to a restaurant in Kyiv where he whipped out his cell phone in the presence of several witnesses and called President Trump. I wish the public could have submitted questions to the committee. If so, it might have gone something like this:

Counsel Castor: Ambassador Sondland, our next question comes from a Mr. Crutchfeld in Gold Ridge, California. Mr. Crutchfeld wants to know what you ordered for lunch at that restaurant in Kyiv on July 26?

Amb. Sondland: Oh, that's easy. It was Chicken Kiev.

Castor: You mean Kyiv? Chicken Kyiv?

Sondland: Po-TAY-toe, po-TAH-toe, counselor.

Castor: Moving on…how would you describe this traditional dish?

Sondland: Oh my, my, my…tender chicken breast, rich butter sauce, a nice crust. Add wild rice and a cold bottle of Chablis, it was…what's the right word?

Castor: Sir?

Sondland: Outlandish! It was outlandish!

Castor: So, you would go back again, for the Chicken Kyiv?

Sondland: Kiev, counselor. And you bet I'd go back. They love my ass over there!

Castor: All righty then. And thank you for that question, Mr. Crutchfeld.

The hearings are not only educational, they can be inspiring. For those of you who are handy in the kitchen, there are many recipes on the Internet for Chicken Kiev. Or Kyiv. Whichever you prefer. It's your chicken.

—R.Q. Crutchfeld

37

Law enforcement officers never receive enough credit for what they do. Putting on a badge every day and going off to serve and protect the community is heroic. In normal times, we take these officers for granted. After all, it's their job, right? We compensate them fairly and provide generous retirement, true? Whatever they face on the job, it's what they signed up for, no?

It is only in extraordinary times we truly appreciate "the thin blue line" that stands between us and chaos. Then and only then do we sing their praises and point them out to our children. *See, Johnny, there goes a real hero. He ran into an active shooter situation and took down the bad guy. She talked a suicide off the ledge and saved a life. They kept the two sides separated at the demonstration, prevented a riot. She took a bullet during a raid on a terrorist cell.*

And yet, there exists a tiny percentage among the ranks that should never be trusted with power, authority, a badge, or a gun. They say power corrupts, but a few come to the job already corrupted. Special Agent Adrian Danforth was one of the corrupt few.

It was a busy Tuesday night at Rosalita's, busy but not overwhelming. Ramona loved Taco Tuesdays because it meant the house filled with familiar faces, those who made it a habit to turn out each week to celebrate the day. She was in the middle of her shift when summoned to the owner's office. She knocked on the door and opened it slowly.

"You wanted to see me, Senora?" She smiled at Rosalita, then noticed a man sitting in a straight-backed chair at the side of the room. He was totally bald, his head gleaming under the fluorescent lights of the office. He looked to be in his forties, dressed in a dark blue suit, striped tie, and gleaming wingtip brogans.

"Yes, Ramona." Rosalita looked concerned. "This is Special Agent Danforth. He is with Immigration Control and Enforcement. He has some questions for you."

Agent Danforth stood and nodded toward Ramona. He reached out with his right hand and offered his business card. She tried to read it but the pulse pounding in her temples made the letters blur.

"Miss Hernandez," he said, "I'm here to ask about your immigration status."

"Immigration status? I don't have an immigration status. I'm an American."

"Really?" Danforth raised his eyebrows.

"Yes 'really'. I was born in Silver City, New Mexico."

Rosalita came to her defense. "I told agent Danforth we have all the proper documentation."

"What's this all about?" Fear and anger fought for Ramona's mind.

"We have a complaint, that you are here illegally and have broken the law." Danforth smiled.

"This is ridiculous. I haven't broken any laws."

Danforth jotted notes on a steno pad. "Okay, here's what I need you to do. I'll be at the Federal offices over by the courthouse through the end of the week. I want you to come in for an interview and bring all necessary documentation—birth certificate, Social Security Card, bank records, tax returns—"

"Bank records? Tax returns?"

"Of course, this is all voluntary at this point, assuming you want to cooperate. I can always get a subpoena if you decide to be uncooperative." Danforth smiled again.

The appointment was set for Saturday morning. Ramona's legs trembled as she returned to work.

⸻

Ramona and Brett were early for the Saturday appointment. They waited in the sterile lobby of the Federal office building on Courthouse Square. The building was a small glass and steel structure, home to several agencies showing the flag in Gold Ridge. At 9:00 a.m., a door opened and Adrian Danforth stepped into the lobby, his wingtips clicking on the marble floor.

"Good morning, Miss Hernandez." He gave Brett a puzzled look. "And you are?"

"This is Brett Corcoran, my boyfriend," Ramona answered.

"Ah, yes. The boyfriend." Danforth looked up at Brett, his smile tightlipped. "Sorry, Mr.—was it Corcoran? You'll have to wait here while I interview Miss Hernandez."

Brett looked at Ramona and shrugged.

Danforth continued, "It shouldn't take long."

Ramona had packed all the materials she thought she'd need in a reusable shopping bag bearing the logo of a local supermarket. She picked up the bag and followed Danforth through the door to the inner sanctum. He led her to a small conference room with an oval table surrounded by eight high-backed chairs. She sat down and placed her bag on the chair next to her.

"Okay, let's get started. First, do you have your birth certificate?"

Ramona rummaged in the bag and handed Danforth the document. He studied it carefully.

"This space here, where the hospital is usually named, there is an address. Why?"

"Because I wasn't born in a hospital. My mom had a midwife. That was our home address."

"Hmm…okay, I see the box for Midwife is checked." He scrutinized the document further. "Mind if I take a snapshot?" He paused. "You know I can subpoena all of your records."

"Go right ahead."

Danforth took the photo with his smart phone. "Did you bring your tax records?"

"Yes, I brought the last three years." She took manila folders from the bag and placed them on the table.

Danforth looked at the Form 1040s and the 1099s that documented income. "I see the 1099 from Rosalita's, but what is this one from the Uptown Gallery?"

"I work there."

"Doing what?"

"I'm a model. For the art classes."

"Okay, and what do you model?"

"I'm a figure model. I model for figure studies, students learning to draw the human body."

"Ah, so you model in the nude?"

"Yes. I'm not the only one, by the way. There are several models around town, men and women."

"Let's cut the crap, Miss Hernandez. Our complaint says you are in the country illegally and you are engaged in prostitution." He waited. "Well…are you? Engaged in prostitution?"

"I am *not*!" Her eyes blazed in anger. "I am a nursing student at Gold Ridge Community College. I pay my bills as a waitress, and as a figure model. And if you suggest one more time that I'm a whore, I'm gonna come over there and slap your face!"

Danforth sat back and stared at her. "That would be assault."

"Or self-defense," she shot back.

Danforth was quiet. He recovered and went on. "Did you bring your bank records?"

Ramona placed several months of bank statements on the table.

"Okay, I see deposits for Rosalita's, and the Uptown Gallery. What are these deposits here?"

"My father sends me some money to help with tuition and books."

"And where are your parents?"

"They live in Roseville." She opened her purse and produced an envelope, a letter from her mother. She pointed to the return address. "Here, this is their home address."

Special Agent Adrian Danforth looked confused. Was the complaint a dud? He busied himself taking snapshots of all the documents Ramona had produced, then asked her to put her things away. He led her back to the lobby where Brett was waiting.

"Thank you for coming in." He spoke in a monotone, avoiding eye contact. "I'll be in touch."

And with that, he was gone.

Ramona and Brett left the building and walked to the parking lot.

"Oh my God. Oh my God, Brett. He asked me if I was a prostitute. He said his complaint said I was illegal and a prostitute." She was shaking, barely able to speak.

"Holy shit! That sonofabitch. No wonder he made me wait in the lobby." Brett was quiet for a moment. "You know what? I smell a rat. A rat named Ralph. I'd bet good money he's the source of this complaint. I should find that little prick and beat the snot out of him."

"No! Absolutely not. That just makes it worse, Brett. Oh God, what am I gonna do? I can't think straight. He has my parents' address and he'll be digging into their lives, too. I've got to call my dad. Right now!" Ramona paused, fighting for control. "What if they're tracking my calls? They can do that, right? Brett, can you call my dad on your phone?"

"Sure, babe." She gave him the number, he keyed it in, pressed Call, and handed her his phone.

Ramona waited as the phone rang. Then she heard the familiar voice. "Papa, it's Ramona. I have something to tell you—"

She began to sob, and she could not stop.

38

Hospice care is overlooked and undervalued, until it touches your family. And then you learn what it means to have a dedicated, caring, professional team guiding you through the final days, hours, minutes of a loved one's life. Afterward, you reflect in amazement at the skill, respect, and empathy, and you ask yourself, *How can they do it? Day after day, one terminal patient after the other. The emotional burden must be immense. Thank God we have such people among us.*

Lilly Morgan headed a team of doctors, nurses, social workers, aides, and bereavement counselors. On a particular Friday night, the team had seen another soul safely on its way. Now it was a question of completing her notes, signing necessary forms, and making sure the equipment and supplies deployed to this grand old home were picked up and returned to the appropriate suppliers. It was a routine she'd completed a hundred times. She was nearly finished when her cell phone rang. She glanced at the screen and saw the name Ted Zane.

Lilly did not answer the call. She placed her elbows on the kitchen table and cupped her head in her hands. Why would Officer Ted Zane of the Gold Ridge Police Department be calling? There was an answer she feared, and so she let the call go to voicemail. Her colleague, Betty, one of the bereavement counselors, approached the table and placed a hand on her shoulder.

"Hey, are you okay?"

Lilly looked up and tried to smile. "Yeah, I'll be fine."

"This was a tough one, wasn't it? Such a sweet lady. It never gets any easier to see them go, does it?"

"You're right, Betty. Thanks…for caring."

Betty patted Lilly's back and walked away.

Lilly stood and walked to the front door and out onto the porch, the night air fresh and cool around her. She pressed the links on her cell phone screen to return Ted Zane's call.

"Hi, Ted. This is Lilly Morgan. Sorry I couldn't answer before."

"Hi, Lilly. Thanks for returning my call." He hesitated. "Look, I hate to be the one to tell you this, but we've got Don down here at the station again. I'm not the one who picked him up this time. Fact is, he's gonna be booked for DUI, Lilly. Nothing I can do to help."

"Oh, God. Is he okay? I mean, other than drinking. Did he hurt himself? Or anyone else, God forbid?"

Ted paused. "Yeah, well, he sideswiped a parked car as the officers were trying to pull him over. So, there's that. And then he got into a beef with the patrolmen. There is talk of resisting arrest, assaulting an officer."

"Oh, Lord, Ted. What should I do? What can I do at this point?"

"Not much, Lilly. He's gonna have to spend the night in a cell. You won't be able to see him until tomorrow morning. He'll be arraigned and released then."

"I don't get it, Ted. He's been doing so well, hasn't had a drink—that I know of—for several weeks. He's been attending AA meetings…" Her voice trailed off.

"We see it all the time, Lilly. Once you're hooked, it's damn hard to quit and make it stick. I'm really sorry, but there's nothing I can do. He's going into the system."

Lilly ended the call and stayed on the porch for a long time, trying to focus, trying to form a plan. She took up her phone again. The first thing to do was to call Brett.

MacKenzie Sherman sat at his desk, staring at a blank page on the notepad in front of him. He intended to make notes preparing for his meeting with Don Corcoran, his Vice President of Marketing. He recalled their prior meeting when he told Corcoran there would be severe consequences for bad behavior related to drinking. Corcoran had assured him there was no problem with alcohol. And now a DUI, a night in jail, suspended license, a stiff fine.

Sherman stood and turned to stare out the window. *Thank God they dropped the resisting arrest and assault charges. So, what's the proper response? Eighteen, almost nineteen years Corcoran's been with the company. First as a sales rep, then as a manager, and finally promotion to Vice President. He's built a strong client base, growing steadily, never outstripping support. The man is very good at his job. Don't overreact. Keep your cool, Mac. Maybe this was the tipping point. Maybe Corcoran is ready for real help. The medical plan provides clinical treatment for addiction. God knows he's earned it. He's a good man. A good man with a big problem. And it all began when his wife died because of the accident. It wasn't his fault. It was nobody's fault. How do you deal with something like that? What if it happened to my Sally? How would I deal with it? No, you've got to help this man. Look what he's done for the Sherman Group, the millions he's brought into the company. Take a deep breath, Mac. A real deep breath.*

The notepad on his desk remained blank.

Don Corcoran paced back and forth in front of his desk, checking his watch every few seconds. He was out of time, due in MacKenzie Sherman's office for the tongue-lashing he so richly deserved. More than that. Old Mac had promised he'd be asked to leave his badge and his keys. There would be the ritual firing, a security guard called to escort him from the building, a perp walk past people he'd worked with for decades, their eyes averted in pity.

He'd packed two large cardboard boxes with personal things, leaving behind drawers and filing cabinets full of company material. There was one last item. He opened a drawer on the right side of his desk, reached behind the file folders and removed a framed eight-by-ten photo of Joanne—young and beautiful, sitting on a beach at Lake Tahoe, smiling at the camera. He stared at the picture for a moment, placed it in his briefcase, closed the lid and snapped the locks. He looked around one last time and headed for the door.

It was a short walk to MacKenzie Sherman's office. Old Mac's secretary smiled as he approached.

"Hi, Don. Mr. Sherman is waiting for you. I'll let him know you're here."

"Don't bother, Janet. I'm going to save him the trouble. Here are my keys to the building, the keys to the company car, the company credit card, and my ID badge."

"Don, wait, you don't want to do it this way—"

"Just tell him I'm saving him the trouble, and me the embarrassment. My personal stuff is in a couple of boxes on my desk. I'll send someone to pick them up later."

"Are you sure about this, Don?"

"Yeah. And, Janet…"

"Yes?"

"Please tell him I said, 'Thanks…for everything.'"

Don turned and walked away toward the elevator, his briefcase in hand. He would summon an Uber driver for a ride home. But first he planned to stop at the Idle Hour, a saloon just down the street. He needed a stiff drink.

39

December 6, 2019

Crusty's Corner

Speaker Nancy Pelosi has authorized the House Judiciary Committee to begin drafting articles of impeachment, setting in motion a process with a foregone conclusion. This playscript is neither a tragedy, nor a comedy. It is a farce. And it may well backfire on Speaker Pelosi and Democrats everywhere who would like to see Donald Trump's presidency come to an end.

We all know what comes next. The Judiciary Committee will approve articles of impeachment. The articles will be transmitted to the Senate where a trial will be conducted. The appointed House managers will make an impassioned case. The President's attorneys will present an impassioned defense. The House managers will propose a motion to present witnesses. The Senate majority, under the firm hand of Mitch McConnell, will defeat the motion. The trial will conclude, a vote will be taken, and President Donald John Trump will be acquitted.

So, what will be gained, or lost? What, if anything, will be changed by this political charade?

One assumes the Democrats hope to sully Trump's image and thereby hurt his standing with independent voters in the 2020 election. They will be keeping a keen eye on the polls in Florida, Pennsylvania, Ohio, Michigan, and Wisconsin. There are other battleground states, but the five mentioned have the electoral votes to swing the election.

The whole shootin' match could explode in the Dems face. First, nothing is going to shake Trump's base. Second, he may emerge with a wave of sympathy, a persecuted president, targeted from day one for resistance and removal. Finally, we are likely to see Trump unchained. Watch for him to seek revenge against anyone who presented testimony against him.

I have great respect for Speaker Pelosi, but I believe she has been pushed by her caucus into a political blunder of historic proportions. Just as Donald Trump will always be remembered as the third president in U.S. history to be impeached, Nancy Pelosi risks being remembered as the speaker who set in motion the process that propelled Trump to four more years.

—R.Q. Crutchfeld

40

Brett sat at the kitchen table with a steaming cup of coffee, dressed in his boxers and a T-shirt. It was just past 7:00 a.m. and he didn't have a class until later that morning. Ramona came into the room and dropped her backpack on the floor, checking her watch, moving quickly. She began to fill a lunch bag with items from the refrigerator: an apple, a carton of yogurt, a small bag of carrot sticks. She was wearing a black crewneck sweater, blue jeans, and tall black leather boots. She came to the table and kissed Brett on the lips, then again, kisses with a promise of more to come.

"I've got to hurry, babe. Early class this morning. What time is your appointment with Dr. Bowman?"

"The usual, 4:00 p.m.," Brett replied.

"Don't forget the *galletas de navidad* we baked for him. They're in the 'Charlie Brown Christmas' tin on the counter." She kissed him again. "Drive carefully. I'll see you tonight."

"You look gorgeous," he called after her. "I love those jeans."

Ramona laughed and hurried out the front door.

Brett tried to play the scene in his mind, rehearsing what he would say to Dr. Bowman. *These cookies are for you and your family, doc. Ramona decorated them. Just to say thank you for everything you've done for me, for... Jeez, what should I say? For all the patience?*

Understanding? Tolerance? I should probably apologize for all the anger and bad attitude I dumped on him. He didn't deserve any of it. Just trying to help.

There was no question the sessions had helped, helped to beat back the night terrors, the anxiety, the anger that threatened to explode over nothing. He still could not watch news reports from Iraq and Afghanistan. And he could not listen to old, gray politicians pontificating about the "mission" in wars that were now a generation old. At least he was no longer tempted to throw a coffee cup through the TV screen.

There was one session that stood out in Brett's mind. Dr. Bowman had complimented him on his progress saying, "You have plans, goals, dreams. You're building a new life, one pitch at a time." One pitch at a time. He liked that.

But there were many people to thank for the progress he'd made. Ramona would top the list. How was he so lucky to love someone who loved him back so fiercely? And Webb, with his infinite patience, good humor, and wisdom. And Joey D. There could be no better friend. Then there was his dad. In spite of all his troubles, Don was the one who found Webb and twisted his arm until he said yes. And of course, Lilly. Without Lilly there would be no Don.

Who was it who said, "It takes a village"? There were a whole lot of *galletas* to bake.

41

Winter break is a time when college ballplayers clean out their lockers and scatter for the holidays. There is Christmas and the New Year to contend with, plus finals and the end of the fall semester. It is a dangerous interlude, a period when it is easy to slack off, ignore the training regimen, add a quick five pounds of holiday cheer.

Unless, of course, your names are Brett Corcoran and Joey DiFranco.

The training partners pushed each other to the max—running, lifting, throwing, hitting indoors in the batting cages. Winter came to the foothills, wet and cold, with an occasional dusting of snow, but it didn't dampen the resolve of Brett and Joey D. Coach Harlon Millburn had assured both of them they had made the team. Brett had his eye on a spot among the top three starting pitchers, and Joey D was making a strong bid to be the leadoff hitter in a decent lineup, and a starter in centerfield or at catcher.

January brought them back to the campus of Gold Ridge Community College, ready to begin a new set of classes, and to gear up for the baseball season ahead. They knew without speaking it aloud: when Coach calls your name, you'd better be ready to execute. The opportunity may not come again.

Ramona Hernandez and Webb Johnson huddled in the grandstand behind home plate at The Nest. It was a cool, overcast January day, the Eagles preparing to play their third game of the new season against the Butte College Roadrunners. Brett Corcoran would be the starting pitcher, Joey DiFranco behind the plate.

The visiting team ran onto the diamond for pregame infield/outfield drills. Ramona turned to Webb with a question.

"Do you think Brett's nervous, Webb?"

"Yeah, sure. It's a good nervous, though. All that adrenaline pumpin', it gets you ready to fight." He paused a beat. "It's a wonder he can concentrate on anything, what with his dad in trouble, losing his job and all."

"Don is talking about rehab, at a place up in Napa County. I hope he's ready."

"So do I, Ramona. Those programs don't come cheap. And it's just a start."

"Lilly has been great. She's been a rock through all of this. Don is lucky to have her."

"She's amazing, all right. What's that old song? 'A good woman is hard to find…'"

Ramona elbowed him gently. "It's 'A good man,' silly. How about you, Webb? Was there a 'good woman' for you?"

"Oh yeah. Once upon a time. I was even married for a while."

"For a while? What happened?"

The visiting team completed its warmups and trotted off the field. The Eagles charged out of the dugout with whoops and whistles for their pregame drills. Webb watched quietly for a few seconds.

"I was drinkin' then. Thought the party would never end. She got fed up with it, told me it was either her or the bottle. Guess which one I chose?"

"Sorry, Webb. I mean, sorry it worked out that way."

"I've made a lot of bad choices, Ramona. And I remember every damn one of 'em."

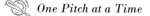

"Don't beat yourself up, Webster Johnson. You're a good man. Look what you've done for Brett." She turned to him and smiled. "He loves you. You know that don't you? He may not say it out loud, but it's true."

"The feelin' is mutual, sugar. He's a fine young man. Don and Joanne did a good job raisin' that boy." Webb glanced her way. "He's lucky to have you, Ramona. Don't know how you do it, with classes and work and all. Brett tells me you're worried about your parents, too. That's quite a load, girl."

"Hey, we're making it work. And don't forget, we've got you on our team." She took his gnarled old hand in hers and gave it a squeeze.

The Eagles finished their pregame routine and trotted back to the dugout. The grounds crew ran out to drag the infield and rake the dirt around the bases. Brett completed his warmups in the bullpen down the left field line while the coaches and umpires met at home plate to exchange lineups and discuss ground rules.

Webb felt a nervous tingle in his belly. *Seventy-nine years old and I still get the damn butterflies.* He reached for the case that held his radar gun.

It was game time.

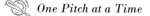

Brett did not pitch poorly. It was a question of command. He had trouble locating his four-seam fastball and often fell behind in the count. His curve ball broke sharply but out of the strike zone, and the hitters wisely ignored it. That left him with two effective pitches: a sinking two-seam fastball and a changeup. Coach Millburn had imposed a seventy-five-pitch limit for these early season, cool weather games, and Brett was done by the end of the fourth inning. The Eagles trailed 2 – 1 when he left. They went on to win the game 5 – 3. Brett was disappointed, but Webb Johnson knew better.

Webb and Ramona caught up with Brett on the way to the locker room after the game. Ramona hooked his left arm, Webb walked on his right side, smiling. Brett looked at him, puzzled.

"What the hell are you smiling about? I didn't have it today, Webb."

"But you learned something, kid. Or at least you should have."

"Yeah? Like what?"

"You're not gonna have your best stuff every time out. In fact, most of the time, there's a pitch or two that just ain't workin'. But you battle through and keep your team close. That's what you did today." The old man smiled again. "You were a pitcher today."

Ramona hugged his arm in agreement.

42

Brett hit the brakes and came to a hard stop at the main entrance to Sutter Roseville Hospital. Ramona jumped out of the car and ran for the door to the lobby. Her mother, waiting inside, caught her in her arms as the doors whooshed open. They held each other, crying softly, reluctant to let go.

"Mama, how is he? Tell me what happened." Ramona led her mother to a bench seat in the lobby, desperate to learn her father's condition.

"He's going to be fine, Ramona. The doctors say it was a heart attack, but he's going to recover. Dry your tears, *mi hija*. Your father is alive."

Consuelo went through all the details of Paul Hernandez's ordeal. A feeling of nausea after dinner. Numbness in his hands. Pain along his jaw line, then a tremendous weight on his chest. The call to 911 and the ambulance ride to the emergency room. And finally, the swift diagnosis. Ramona tried and failed to control her tears as the story unfolded.

"Can I see him?"

"He's in the cardiac ICU. They may let you see him for a minute. Let's go up. Uncle Fred and Aunt Imelda are there in the waiting room."

Ramona could see her father, but only through the window of the Intensive Care Unit. What she saw shocked her: the tubes, the IV drip, the blood pressure cuff, and all the blinking, beeping machines. As a nursing student, she'd seen it all before, but never attached to someone she loved.

The family kept its vigil through the night, sustained by vending machine coffee and snacks. As night turned to morning, Fred and Imelda excused themselves and headed for home, just a few miles away. Brett closed his eyes and tried to power nap. Consuelo took her daughter aside for a conversation.

"Listen, *mi hija*, there's something you must know."

"What is it, Mama?" Ramona braced herself for bad news.

"Even before this happened, your father and I made a decision. We cannot live under this cloud of stress and fear, expecting a knock on our door at any hour. You know ICE has been poking around, digging into our background. This Agent Danforth, the one who questioned you, had us in for an interrogation. We are worried— no, terrified—that he will find the holes in our story, find that we are here illegally. Our documents are not near so secure as yours. We could be arrested, hauled from our home, placed on a flight to Mexico City, or some other place strange to us."

"I'm so sorry, Mama. It is my fault, this man Danforth and all the terrible things he brings to you—"

"Stop it now, Ramona. It is not your fault. It is something we are responsible for, something we have lived with for twenty-three years since we came here with you as an infant."

"What are you telling me, Mama? What are you going to do?"

"Your father and I are going to return to Mexico."

"Oh God, no!"

"Yes, *hija*, it is the only way. We have cousins in Puerto Vallarta. They've done well in the hotel business, the tourist trade. They say it is a lovely city, for the most part. They have work for us, managing their properties. All we need is to get your Papa well—"

"Mama, you're saying you will self-deport? It's so unfair."

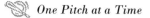

"Uncle Fred will purchase our home. He'll sell what we don't need and ship the rest to us. We have savings and good equity in the house, and he will wire the money to us. We will be fine in Puerto Vallarta."

"But what about the cartel? What if they come after Papa?"

"We will be far across the country from Matamoros, far from the gulf cartel. Besides, it has been more than twenty years and Papa is no longer a journalist. We will be safe on the West Coast."

Ramona fell into her mother's arms, her weeping uncontrolled.

"Listen to me, Ramona. It will be fine. We'll get your Papa well, get him strong again, all the worry and the stress will fall away. And you and Brett will visit us. There are direct flights. You'll come and stay and enjoy the sun and you'll help me make tamales—"

Consuelo's voice broke and her tears fell on her daughter's shoulder. There was only so much she could say to make the train wreck seem like a parade.

43

March 8, 2020

Crusty's Corner

For several weeks, we've been following reports out of Wuhan, China, about what is being called the *novel* coronavirus. Novel in the sense that it is unknown, we have no vaccine, and no therapeutics. China's handling of the outbreak, the genesis of which was a jump from animal to human, is being viewed with skepticism. Was there an attempt at a cover up?

Our public health officials have issued assurances the virus is no threat to U.S. citizens. Now we learn from neighboring Placer County that on March 4, an elderly resident died—and tested positive for COVID-19, the disease caused by the virus.

It seems the link to Placer County is the cruise ship *Grand Princess*. The deceased resident took a cruise to Mexico on the *Princess* in February. As of this writing, nineteen crew members and two passengers have tested positive for the coronavirus.

Test kits had to be airlifted to the ship off the California coast. There are 3,533 passengers and crew onboard.

On March 6, Vice President Mike Pence announced the ship would be brought to a non-commercial port where all passengers will be quarantined and tested.

Mike's boss, however, has a different take on the situation. President Trump prefers the ship remain at sea. Why? Because he "…likes the numbers where they are." He doesn't want a possible doubling of the confirmed cases in the U.S.

Consider the impact on the Stock Market, for goodness sake!

The President needs to understand one irreversible fact: the novel coronavirus has already disembarked.

—R.Q. Crutchfeld

44

It was a fair day for an auction, no rain in the forecast, blue sky peeking through thin white clouds, temperature in the upper fifties. "Estate Sale," screamed the announcements on Craig's List, Facebook, and Instagram. "Everything must go." Chairs, tables, sofas. Headboards, mattresses, dressers. A pool table with a half-dozen cues. Pots, pans, dishes, cups, silverware. "Highest quality, Lowest prices." Linens, towels, pillows. Appliances of all shapes and sizes. Artwork, including signed and numbered prints. "Open for viewing at noon. Auction begins 1:00 p.m. sharp."

Don Corcoran stood with the auctioneer as the last items were taken from the house and placed in the long, circular driveway or the garage. The auctioneer's podium was set up on the front steps, the sound system powered by a long extension trailing into the house.

"Well, Mr. Corcoran, looks like we are ready to go. If the weather holds, I think we'll have a good crowd."

"Yeah. Hope so." Don surveyed a lifetime of *stuff* he and Joanne had accumulated. None of it seemed to mean much now, except for the money it might yield. He would be moving into Lilly's apartment far across town, under her watchful eye, at least until it was time to enter the rehabilitation facility they had selected. He'd been sober since the day he walked away from his job at The Sherman Group, but he'd kill for a cold beer right now. *Just one glass for thirst. Maybe one more for taste. That's all I need.*

"Have you decided what to do with the items that don't sell, Mr. Corcoran?"

"Yeah, I'll either donate what's left, or leave it for the new owners. Escrow will close in about thirty days."

The man looked at the multi-page list of items to be auctioned. "I think you'll do real well. This is all quality merchandise, the best I've dealt with in a while."

Don saw a couple of cars approaching on the narrow access road. The serious buyers would arrive early, followed by the Looky Lou's. "Okay, I'm gonna disappear and leave it to you and your team. I'll be downstairs in the rec room if you need me. And you have my cell number if there are any questions."

"Right, Mr. Corcoran. Just relax. You're in good hands." The man smiled and waved as Don walked away.

He made his way down the stairs to the room once cluttered with toys and gadgets. Now there remained a large flat-screen TV, a DVD player, and one overstuffed chair. He browsed through his collection of classic movies: *On the Waterfront; Casablanca; An Officer and a Gentleman; The Cincinnati Kid.* He selected *Bull Durham,* stuffed it into the machine and hit the play button. He smiled at Annie Savoy's opening line: "I believe in the Church of Baseball…"

Don's mind wandered as the familiar opening scenes unfolded on the screen. *Lilly. Where would I be without Lilly? Probably dead by now.* At her insistence, they'd built a plan, one that held a future for the two of them, a life worth living, a love worth getting sober for. He would enter rehab, a program scheduled for a minimum forty-five days. After that, he'd go back to AA with Webb Johnson, the support and reinforcement vital for his resolve. And he'd begin to look for a job. He needed work to feel complete and useful, a productive member of society. There had to be companies out there that would appreciate his track record with Sherman. After all, he'd been a top-level executive, a consistent producer, a star. Money would not be a problem, not for the foreseeable future. He'd done well at Sherman, very well. There were savings, a rich 401k with company match, good equity from the sale of the house, and he was vested in Sherman's retirement program for the future. And he would have Lilly. None of it meant much without her, his rock, his anchor, the firm handhold that kept him from falling off the mountain.

Annie Savoy finished her soliloquy: "I've tried 'em all, I really have, and the only church that truly feeds the soul, day in, day out, is The Church of Baseball."

Don's attention was drawn back to the screen as Max Patkin, The Clown Prince of Baseball, performed his routine to Bill Haley's "Rock Around the Clock."

Sixty miles away, at Sacramento International Airport, Ramona said goodbye to her parents. Paul and Consuelo would board a flight bound for Puerto Vallarta and their new life. Uncle Fred and Aunt Imelda were on hand to wish them Godspeed and to assure that all business with the sale of their home and possessions was well in hand.

Tears flowed as Ramona hugged her parents and promised to visit as soon as spring semester and graduation were completed. She would have to prepare for the exam to become a Registered Nurse, but the trip to Puerto Vallarta would be a graduation gift from the family. She tried to put a happy face on the prospect—but failed completely.

How could this be happening? Her father suffering a heart attack, her parents terrified by an ICE investigation, the decision to self-deport and start over in Mexico, too afraid even to stay and see her graduate. It was a nightmare, and it kept getting worse.

The sign read, "Ticketed passengers only beyond this point." Ramona could go no farther with her parents. They would board the tram that would carry them to the TSA security checkpoints and on to the boarding gates.

"I love you, Mama. I love you, Papa. Call as soon as you land, okay?" Ramona's attempt at bravery was betrayed by the tears streaming down her face.

Paul and Consuelo held her close, talking over themselves. "*Mi hija, mi corazon, mi alma*, be safe, be well, study hard, make us proud, as you have always made us proud. Do not worry for us, we will be fine, we will be with family. God bless you..."

The doors to the tram slid shut and the shuttle began to roll away. Aunt Imelda gathered Ramona in her arms. Uncle Fred waved and blinked back tears.

The few remaining items from Don's estate sale had been moved into the three-car garage. He was surprised the pool table was among them, sure it would have been the first to sell. He rolled a ball across the surface, watched it career off the rails, and saw that it was reasonably level. He racked the balls, chose a cue, and began a game of 8-ball against himself. He would take the solid balls, his alter ego the stripes. The check from the auctioneer was tucked into his shirt pocket, the proceeds not bad, though they represented pennies on the dollar from the original purchase prices. Alter Ego sank the 11-ball as his cell phone began to chime. It was Lilly calling.

"Hi, honey. How did it go?"

"Not bad. Just a handful of stuff left over. We moved it into the garage."

"Is everyone gone?"

"Yeah."

"What are you doing?"

"Playing one last game of pool. You can guess who's winning." He laughed.

"Come on home, sweetie. I'm making the pasta dish you love, the one with Havarti cheese and kalamata olives. A nice salad, lots of garlic bread. Sound good?"

"Sounds great. Want me to pick up—" He started to say, *A nice bottle of Cabernet*, but he caught himself.

"Just come home, baby. Okay?"

"Okay, love. Soon as I finish this game."

Don slammed the 8-ball into a corner pocket. He set the cue on the table, closed the garage door, and walked to his car. He turned to take one last look at what was once his dream home.

Joanne had furnished and decorated their nest with exquisite taste and love, her touch everywhere you looked. She was also the family photographer, capturing special moments to be framed, mounted, and admired by all: Brett as a newborn, the classic nudie proudly displaying his dimpled butt; Brett taking his first steps, or dressed in his first Little League uniform, or in a suit and tie bound for his first prom. Very few shots of Joanne. She preferred to be behind the camera. The few that existed caught her beauty and her spirit, the gleam in her eye that made her so special. Now the house was empty, the walls bare, as though none of it ever happened.

Don heard a car approaching behind him. He turned to see Brett park and exit his vehicle just beyond the driveway. The two men locked eyes and then walked toward each other, meeting halfway.

"Hey…I didn't expect to see you, son."

"Just got off work. Lilly called, told me you were here."

"I'm glad you came."

Brett embraced his father and held him tight. "Sorry, Dad. I'm really sorry."

"Me too, son. I really blew it. Blew it big-time. Can you forgive me?"

"I love you, Dad. Come on, I'll follow you to Lilly's place."

45

Some refer to it as *being in the zone*, or *experiencing flow*. Others call it *mojo*, or *juju*. Whatever it is called, it is a rare happening for an athlete and you can never count on it, because it's as fickle as the wind. If it happens to a golfer, every shot is flushed, and every putt finds the bottom of the cup. For a tennis player, all strokes are smooth precision, the ball explodes from the racket, and placement is perfection. In basketball, suddenly a player's fingertips are magic and he or she can't miss, no matter where the shot is launched.

And then there is baseball. For a pitcher, the ball leaps from his hand, velocity is effortless, breaking pitches snap under the hitter's bat, and if contact is made, it's weak, soft, puny. Think of Christy Matthewson's brilliance in the 1905 World Series. Think of Don Larson's perfect game in 1956. Think of Nolan Ryan's seven no-hitters. It isn't often you find yourself *in the zone* or *experiencing flow*. All you can do is thank God and pray it will last.

Brett Corcoran had the feeling as he warmed up in the bullpen for a home game against the Sierra College Wolverines. He could not miss a target. His curve was wicked sharp. His fastball sizzled. *Oh, baby! Take this shit to the bump, Corcoran. Don't leave it here in the pen. Okay, one more pitch and you're ready. Fastball, glove side, knees. Bam! That's it, let's go. Thank you, God. Thank you thank you thank you.* He put on his warmup jacket against the cool February air and headed for the dugout. *Game on!*

———————

There are times when the *mojo* stays in the bullpen and refuses to enter the game. Or it may last a few innings and then disappear. There are no guarantees. On this particular day, the magic stayed with Brett as he took his warmup pitches for the first inning. He felt like Superman. He looked into the grandstand at The Nest and found Webb Johnson seated with the scouts in the section behind home plate. *Watch this, Coach. Let's see how long it lasts.*

Brett was out of the first inning on twelve pitches, including two strikeouts. The second and third innings were more of the same; the hitters who made contact recorded weak outs. After six innings, Brett had faced the minimum eighteen batters. He began to take notice as he sat in the dugout between innings. No one spoke to him, no one even sat close, not even Joey D, his catcher, who would normally sit down to discuss the hitters they'd face next.

Oh my God! I've got a perfect game going. Brett laughed out loud. This was so old school! Did guys still do this? Avoid the pitcher like a plague during a no-hit, no-run game? He thought that superstition died years ago. He wanted to laugh and shout, "Hey, no-hitter, no-hitter, no-hitter!" That would break the ice for sure. Instead he bit his lip. He would respect his teammates and not spoil their fun.

The Eagles broke through with a run on back-to-back doubles in the bottom of the sixth. Brett went to the mound for the top of the seventh with a 1 – 0 lead. He set the visitors down 1-2-3 to remain perfect through seven innings.

Joey D tripled to start the bottom of the seventh for the Eagles, then scored on a soft ground ball to the second baseman. Now the lead was 2 – 0.

Brett faced the fourth, fifth, and sixth hitters in the top of the eighth and set them down in order. Perfect through eight.

The Eagles did not score in their half of the eighth. Brett went to the mound for the top of the ninth. He'd face the last three hitters in the Wolverines order. No one had spoken to him since the fifth inning.

The leadoff hitter popped up to short for the first out. The next batter was a lefty with a smooth swing that recalled Ken Griffey, Jr. Brett jumped out to an 0 – 2 count with a four-seam fastball on the outside corner at the knees, followed by a sharp curve that caught the inside corner at the letters. His next pitch, a two-seam fastball inside at the knees just missed. With the count 1 – 2, Joey D called for a changeup away. Brett placed it perfectly with good movement. The hitter stroked a line drive to left field for a base hit.

The perfect game bubble had burst.

The sparse crowd began to rise, one or two at a time until it was unanimous, to give Brett a standing ovation. Brett smiled and nodded in recognition to the hitter standing on first base. Joey D trotted to the mound for a temperature check.

"Hey, man, that was some ride. You okay?"

"Yeah, Joey. I'm good."

"Okay, don't lose focus. This is the tying run at the plate. We need two outs to get 'er done, buddy. Got it?"

"Yeah, I got it." Brett took a deep breath.

The number nine hitter, a well-built right hander, stepped into the box and pounded the plate with his bat. Brett's second pitch was a two-seamer with nice sink that produced a ground ball to the second baseman who fielded it cleanly. It became a 4-6-3 double play.

Game over.

Brett had faced the minimum twenty-seven hitters, striking out twelve. He'd thrown 120 pitches through nine innings. It would go into the books as a one-hit shutout, without question the best game he'd ever pitched. His teammates crowded around to slap his back and offer congratulations. They lined up to shake hands with the visiting team and then headed for the locker room. Brett looked for

Webb and found him surrounded by scouts in the stands, answering all the obvious questions. *Yes, the young man had come a long way. Yes, he definitely had his A-game today. Yes, the mid-nineties fastball was his best pitch.* And so it went.

Brett waited for the crowd to clear away, then hurried to embrace his Yoda.

46

March 24, 2020

Crusty's Corner

President Trump today proposed novel remedies for the novel coronavirus: ultraviolet light taken inside the body; and/or injection of disinfectants. One can only wonder: Is the President wearing down, becoming disoriented? That would be understandable at his age.

Regarding the ultraviolet light, could he be thinking of colonoscopy? Doesn't the colonoscope put a little light where the sun doesn't shine? Not that it kills any viruses while it's in there; but still, it's easy to get these things confused.

Just as the press briefing ended, I received an email from a friend. Attached to the message was an image of a very realistic looking bottle labeled "Clorox Chewables." A small banner at the bottom of the label read, "Don't die. Maybe." This is a classic example of our ability to turn any statement by a politician into an instant joke.

I mean, let's face it: Clorox Chewables is *funny*!

On the other hand (as Tevye would say), this is no laughing matter. These statements are coming from POTUS, the Commander in Chief, the Leader of the Free World. This man walks around with the keys to our nuclear arsenal in his pocket.

Think about that for a minute.

I suggest we wait until tomorrow and give President Trump the wiggle room to say, "Hey, just kidding, folks. I wanted to see if you were paying attention."

In the meantime, please do not send me an image of Lysol Gummies.

—R.Q. Crutchfeld

47

At first it was a rumor. It became an alert, a dire warning, a declared emergency, a global pandemic, an alarm bell clanging in the night with red lights flashing. It was christened the *novel* coronavirus, which sounds rather whimsical. Why *novel*? Why not *unique, unknown, unprecedented, exotic*? Why not *deadly*? Along the way, people who should have known better declared it to be no threat to Americans.

We've got this. No worries. It's contained.
Look at the stock market, an all-time high.
When the weather gets warm, maybe April, it will disappear.
There are fifteen cases. Soon, it will be zero.

John Donne wrote, "No man is an island..." Neither is a country.
In Gold Ridge in the Sierra foothills in Northern California, the proper folks were paying attention. The word spread through the Board of Directors at Whispering Pines Community Hospital.

What about this report, this thing *in Wuhan, China?*
Ah, that's China. Let them deal with it. It's not coming here.
But viruses don't respect borders.

Hey, listen to Dr. Fauci. He says it poses no threat to U.S. citizens.
Well…if Fauci says so. Just the same, let's take inventory.
How many respirators? What's our supply level in PPE? How
many ICU beds do we have? How do we get test kits?
You're overreacting, but we'll get the info for you.

No man is an island. Neither is an isolated town in the foothills.

Oh my God! Did you hear about the case at UC Davis?
Yeah, and cases in Santa Clara County. Too close to home, for sure.
People are dying. One of them at Kaiser in
Roseville. Roseville, for God's sake!

No man—or woman—is an island.

Ramona and Brett walked across the quad at Gold Ridge Community College, heading for their vehicles in the parking lot. Each carried a backpack full of books and binders. Brett lugged a large equipment bag stuffed with baseball gear.

"So, what happens now?" Brett's face was a mask of concern.

"I'm not sure. My instructors are going to try to do online classes, but they've never done them before. We all left our contact information and they promised to be in touch. My clinical requirements are the most important to me—actually working at the hospital. They are going to try to make sure that happens. There's talk that if we can at least complete our clinicals, we'll be able to graduate in June." She paused. "How 'bout you?"

"I didn't hear much about remote classes, but instructors said they'd be in touch. As for baseball, the season is shut down. Coach Millburn doesn't know if it will restart, but he didn't sound optimistic. I mean, we may be done." He adjusted his grip on the equipment bag. "How about work?"

"Rosalita's is closed, but she's going to try to set up curbside take-out, maybe delivery with GrubHub or DoorDash. All of that would be with a skeleton crew. Looks like I'm out of a job."

"Yeah, Big-5 is locked down, too. I'm gonna have to scramble around, try to find some kind of gig."

They walked along in silence, watching their fellow students vacate the campus.

"I feel really bad, Brett. You were off to such a great start, I mean the near-perfect game, all the scouts there eating it up."

"Yeah, well, no point in crying about it. Remember what Tom Hanks said, 'There's no crying in baseball.'" He laughed. "Anyway, Joey D and I are gonna continue to work out and try to stay in shape. Joey was off to great start, too."

"What about the Major League draft? Doesn't that happen in June?"

"Yeah, but there's talk that it may be only ten rounds. Maybe even less. No point in drafting guys if they have no place to play."

They reached the parking lot and loaded the bags into their respective vehicles.

"I've got to stop by Rosalita's and pick up my check." Ramona stood on tiptoes for a quick kiss.

"Okay. I'm going to go by Lilly's and check on Dad. His rehab is on hold while the facility gets approval to stay open. See you at home." Brett turned and scanned the campus, wondering when it would reopen and if he'd ever be back.

Brett unlocked the apartment door and stepped inside. He dropped his backpack near the door. He could hear water running in the bathroom. Ramona opened the door and popped her head out.

"Hi. How was your dad?"

"He's okay. A little jumpy, but okay."

"Good. Hey, I picked up some cloth masks for us. They're on the counter."

"Yeah, I see 'em."

"I'm gonna take a shower. Come wash my back, okay?"

Brett smiled. "Best offer all day."

The bathroom was filled with steam when he opened the door. He stepped into the shower stall wearing one of the masks left on the counter, baby blue in color, white loops hooked around his ears.

Ramona laughed. "Who was that masked man? I wanted to thank him."

"Don't know. But he left this."

"Oh my! Now, that's what I call a silver bullet!"

Shelter in Place wasn't all bad.

Ramona moved around the kitchen, assembling the ingredients for a quick supper. She wore a robe cinched tight at the waist, her hair, still damp from the shower, pulled back in a ponytail. They'd decided on scrambled eggs and toast, about as simple as it gets. She cracked the eggs and began to whisk them in a mixing bowl as Brett entered the kitchen. He came up behind her, wrapped her in his arms and kissed the back of her head.

"Before you cook those eggs, I need you for a minute."

She laughed. "Oh my God. You're ready again, so soon?"

"No, not that. But keep that thought." He took her hand and led her to a chair at the kitchen table. "There's something I need to talk to you about."

"Okay...what is it, babe?"

"It's just...I mean, it seems like everything is up for grabs right now. Nothing is sure, nothing is certain. Know what I mean?"

"Yes. Yes, I do."

"So, I want there to be one thing in this world that is fixed and solid and beyond question. Something to depend on." He reached in the pocket of his jeans and placed a ring box on the table. He opened the lid to reveal a diamond ring, a beautiful pear-shaped stone in a simple setting.

Ramona gasped. Brett got down on one knee in front of her.

"This was my mom's ring." He paused and swallowed hard. "Ramona Hernandez, will you marry me?" He took the ring from the box and offered it to her.

"Oh my God! Are you sure? Your mom's ring?" Her hands covered her face, tears spilling down her cheeks.

"My dad says he'd be honored if you wore it." Brett's voice trembled; his eyes welled. "By the way, I spoke to your father. He gave us his blessing."

"Of course, I'll marry you, Brett Corcoran. Yes, yes, yes!"

"Whatever happens from now on, it's you and me, together."

The eggs went uncooked, the bread untoasted. There were more important things to do.

48

Gold Ridge, with its mild climate and pine forest ambience, was a popular location for congregate facilities, and nursing homes became the first COVID-19 hot spots. Some patients arrived at Whispering Pines Community Hospital accompanied by caretakers or family members. Others came by ambulance after a call to 911. It did not take long for the ten ICU beds to fill up and the supply of ventilators to run low.

Staff members from the care facilities were the next wave and the hospital administrators faced the sickening realization that the virus was out in the community, circulating unchecked. Drastic measures were required.

The hospital was divided into COVID and non-COVID wings, the sections sealed off with plastic sheeting and duct tape. All personnel in the COVID area were required to wear full PPE, including masks and face shields. It immediately became clear that the burn rate on protective equipment would exhaust supplies on hand within a week or ten days. Urgent searches were launched to find suppliers with N95 masks, gloves, gowns, face shields, and ventilators. And, of course, test kits. *Where in the hell do we get test kits, and how do we get them processed?* A call went out to the community for people with nursing experience, currently inactive or retired, to step up in the crisis.

All hands on deck. STAT!

Lilly Morgan answered the call. The hospice organization she worked for released her to work at the hospital where her long years of experience were needed. She became a leader in the admissions area, guiding the triage required to prioritize and direct patients to the proper level of care.

Ramona was part of the next wave to step up. The nursing program at the community college worked with the hospital to involve the twelve students scheduled to graduate in June. The student nurses would staff the non-COVID wings, freeing veteran RN's to work on the COVID side. In return, the students would receive full credit toward clinical requirements.

The community was at war against the insidious enemy—and it was losing. Bodies began to accumulate in the small morgue in the hospital basement, waiting for families to come forward and claim them. *What do we do when we run out of space? Can we get a refrigerated trailer out back?*

The toll on the doctors, nurses, and support staff was horrendous. *These people die alone. No one can see them, to say I love you, to say goodbye.* Add to that the fear of going home, spreading the disease to family. They pleaded with administrators. *Put us up in a hotel. Isolate us. Don't make us take this home.* The bosses listened, hoping and praying funds would materialize to pay the bills. War is hell.

───✺───

Lilly was nearing the end of a twelve-hour shift, exhausted, thinking only of a warm meal and a few hours of sleep. Two ambulances arrived at the emergency entrance bringing new patients. She stood next to Dr. Peter Chung, the emergency room physician, as the automatic doors whooshed open. Lilly knew Dr. Chung looked all of eighteen years old without an N95 mask and face shield. Now only his gentle brown eyes were visible. He was a take-charge presence in the ER, just what was needed.

"Okay, bring them in. What have we got?" Dr. Chung listened to the EMT's report, took vital signs, listened carefully with his stethoscope, then barked instructions to a couple of orderlies. "This one is a candidate for intubation. Get a chest X-ray, then up to Intensive Care."

Lilly glanced at the second gurney as it was wheeled through doors. "Oh my God. Oh my God!" Her face shield fogged with each breath.

"What? What is it?" Dr. Chung turned to her.

"I know this man." Lilly bent close to the old man on the gurney. "Webb. Webb, it's me—Lilly." She reached with her gloved hand to squeeze his forearm.

"Lilly—" His voice was faint and tired.

"Okay, Webb, we've got you. We're gonna take care of you." She stepped aside for the young doctor to do his thing.

"Okay," he said. "We've seen worse. Chest X-ray then get him upstairs. Get him started on oxygen and an IV. Let's move."

Lilly repeated herself. "We're gonna take care of you, Webb." At least he recognized her through the mask and the shield. *Oh, sweet Jesus. I've got to call Brett and Ramona, first chance I get. Should I call Don? Maybe not. Damnit, I'm too tired to think.*

⌒〜⌒

Ramona hurried home at the end of her shift. She stripped to her underwear in the hallway while Brett held a beach towel to shield her. She stuffed her clothes into a plastic bag, then ran to the shower to scrub herself from head to toe. She was just out of the shower when Brett's cell phone rang.

"Brett, it's Lilly. Is Ramona with you?"

"Yeah, she's right here."

"I have news you'll both want to hear."

"Wait a sec, I'll put it on speaker. There. Can you hear me?"

"Yeah. Brace yourselves. We admitted Webb Johnson tonight."

Brett and Ramona gasped in tandem.

Brett recovered first. "How is he? Is it bad?"

"All the classic symptoms—low oxygen, coughing, elevated temp, difficulty breathing. I've seen worse come through the door, but I won't sugarcoat it. It doesn't look good."

"Will he have to be intubated? Go on a ventilator?" Ramona stared at the phone.

"He's right on the edge. They're trying a cocktail of therapeutics, but nobody knows how the virus will respond."

Brett asked the question, even though he knew the answer. "Can we see him?"

"No. Nobody is allowed in. I've checked on him, but he's been out cold. He did recognize me and say my name when they brought him in. We've had two or three admissions from that place where he lives, the Bitter Creek Hotel. Seems to be a hotspot."

"Keep an eye on him, Lilly. And if you catch him awake, give him our love." Brett's eyes welled, his voice choked.

"Listen, you two, I need your advice. I'm so out of it I can't think straight. Should I tell Don about Webb's condition?"

Brett and Ramona stared at each other. Brett said, "Are you going home after your shift, Lilly?"

"No. They have a room for me at the Truro. I don't want to risk taking it home. It's midnight, but Don is up, waiting for my call. What do you think?"

"Let me call him," Brett said. "And I'll drive over there and stay with him, make sure he is okay."

It felt strange to treat Don Corcoran like a fragile teacup, easily broken, prone to fall off the edge and shatter at the slightest provocation. But that's where they were. The three conspirators agreed to Brett's plan and ended the call.

49

April 26, 2020
Crusty's Corner
I've been hoping to publish a specific column. It goes like this:

President Donald J. Trump announced today that he, in conjunction with his Coronavirus Task Force, is taking full charge of the federal government's response to the pandemic. Under the authority of the Defense Production Act, he and his team will order production of critical equipment and materials, including ventilators, gowns, masks, gloves, and shoe coverings. And, all materials required to drive testing, including swabs, tubes, reagents, and analytic machines will be produced under the same authority. Manufacture of these items will be assigned to iconic American companies, including Ford, General Motors, Johnson & Johnson, Dupont, 3M, and many others. Labels will read, "Made in the U.S.A."

The strategic stockpile of material and equipment will be acquired by the government at a fair value per unit that covers cost and assures a small profit for the producers. The stockpile will be gathered and stored in warehouses located in Kansas City. The Army Corp of Engineers will oversee inventory and take charge of shipping and distribution to hot spots throughout the country, supported by the U.S. Air Force. Governors of each state will be able to purchase supplies as needed from the strategic stockpile at price levels consistent with those that existed prior to the pandemic.

The CDC will step forward, as in past crises, and issue mandatory guidelines and best practices for meat packing plants, prisons, and elder care facilities. CDC will also issue enforceable guidelines for reopening all segments of society—schools, houses of worship, business offices, restaurants, casinos, professional sports, bars, and so on. Finally, the CDC will draft a National Testing Strategy to identify and treat the infected, contact-trace and isolate the exposed.

In other words, the federal government will apply every lesson learned in the first wave of the pandemic to respond forcefully if there is a new peak or a second wave.

A policy declaration will be written and signed by the President, with commemorative pens distributed to the members of his team. In the historic photo of this event, *all* participants will be wearing face masks.

And there you have it, the column I really want to publish. I'll keep this draft in my drawer—just in case.

—R.Q. Crutchfeld

50

Lilly was back on duty the next afternoon, relieved to find a quiet period in the ER. She went to a phone and called the nurse's station upstairs in the ICU to check on Webb. The news was not encouraging.

"His breathing is worse, oxygen level dropping. We have a ventilator for him. He'll likely be intubated within the hour." The charge nurse was direct, concise.

"Okay, thanks. I'll check back later." She placed the handset in its cradle, closed her eyes and said a prayer. *God, watch over that sweet old man. Don't take him from us.*

There was a commotion outside the door to the ER. An ambulance had arrived and EMTs were scurrying around, unloading a gurney, rushing a patient toward the door as it opened with the familiar whoosh. Lilly heard the EMTs speaking, passing information to the ER physician. "Sherman," they said. "Sally Sherman." Lilly recognized the name—the wife of MacKenzie Sherman, President of The Sherman Group. *Oh my God. Sally Sherman, presenting at the hospital where the new wing is named for her and her husband.* Lilly could see the prominent citizen, a woman in her sixties, was in distress, laboring to breathe. The physician's exam was swift and she was on her way, headed for the ICU. Lilly's heart raced, her pulse pounded at her temples. *Rich or poor, doesn't matter. This damn virus will find you.*

An hour later, quiet fell on the ER, all patients stable, well-attended. Lilly decided a cup of coffee was in order. She headed for the break room. Dr. Chung was there, using a pair of tongs to pluck a donut from a large pink box, his face shield and mask set aside for the moment. He looked at Lilly, his young face pinched in concern.

"Lilly, why are you wearing a surgical mask? Where is your N95?"

"They're running short and they needed the N95s upstairs in the ICU."

"That's not good. You need an N95 in the ER. Track one down, tell them I said so."

"Okay, I'll get on it." *So much for a cup of coffee.* She left the break room and headed toward the elevator. *Two birds with one stone. I'll get an N95 upstairs and check on Webb while I'm there.*

The elevator doors opened on the third floor and Lilly stepped up to the nurses' station. "Johnson? Webster Johnson?"

The nurse checked her computer screen. "He's in number five." She motioned to her left.

Lilly walked down the hall toward unit five. Suddenly, alarms began to sound, multiple electronic devices announcing trouble. She ran the final steps to the cubicle and rushed inside.

"Webb! Webb, can you hear me?" The monitor next to the bed registered no pulse. She leaned close, her ear next to his nose and mouth. He was not breathing. *Chest compressions. Now!* She tried to administer compressions but could not get leverage. She leapt onto the bed, her face shield flying off and clattering to the floor. She straddled Webb's narrow body, put her left hand on top of her right, fingers interlocked, and pressed hard on the center of his chest. She knew the drill: one hundred compressions per minute. Go! "One, two, three, four, five, —"

The room began to fill with men and women in full protective gear, one of the women calling instructions in a firm voice. Strong hands helped Lilly from the bed and moved her to the side of the room. The trauma team worked furiously for several minutes while alarms buzzed and beeped in crescendo. And then the woman who had taken charge straightened up, looked around the room, and calmly reached out to silence the alarms. The room went still.

"He's gone. Nothing we can do." A photo pinned to her protective gown read, *Hi, I'm Doctor Patel.* She walked to where Lilly was standing. "Are you okay, Miss—?"

"Morgan. Lilly Morgan. I'm an RN." Her voice trembled, she blinked back tears.

"Did you know this man, Nurse Morgan?"

"Yes. Yes, I did. He was…he was family." Lilly began to gather herself, shock losing ground to anger. "What happened here? Can you explain this?"

"What do you mean?" The doctor's tone was cold.

"I mean, he was supposed to go on a ventilator more than an hour ago. There's no ventilator in here. What happened?"

"We had to make a choice. The vent went to another patient."

A picture flashed in Lilly's mind, the scene in the ER, the frantic response when Sally Sherman was admitted. Was that it? Was Mrs. Sherman, with her name engraved on the building, the "other" patient? Lilly wanted to scream, *And who exactly was that patient?* But the words would not come, because she did not want to know the answer. She could not live with the idea Webb was a casualty of white privilege.

Dr. Patel stared at Lilly. "Where is your face shield?"

"It fell off—"

"And you're wearing a surgical mask? No N95?"

"We ran short."

"You were doing chest compressions wearing only a surgical mask. You just exposed yourself to COVID-19." Dr. Patel paused to let it sink in. "You are going into quarantine. For fourteen days. Starting now. Come with me."

The doctor led Lilly out of the room and down the hall, destination unknown. Lilly knew two things for sure: This damn virus will find you, and Webb Johnson was dead.

51

By Mother's Day, the patterns of contagion were clear. Nursing homes and elder care facilities were hotspots. So were meat processing plants, and prisons, even U.S. Navy ships. Some states began publishing statistics—confirmed infections, deaths—for at-risk facilities. Others decided not to, because if the public doesn't know the truth, the truth can't be a political liability. Politics trumped public health. But you did not have to be in a nursing home, meat processing plant, prison, or the Navy to get sick and die. This virus would find you.

Case in point, the following report from the *Sacramento Bee*:

Iconic 'newsboy' succumbs to COVID-19

Robert Quinn Crutchfeld, known affectionately as Crusty Bob, passed away yesterday at the age of eighty-four. It has been confirmed he died of COVID-19 after being admitted to Whispering Pines Community Hospital in Gold Ridge.

For more than forty years, Mr. Crutchfeld was the owner/publisher/editor of the *Beacon*, a weekly newspaper distributed every Friday morning in Gold Ridge and the surrounding foothill communities.

His fiercely independent world view allowed him to skewer the arrogant and powerful on both sides of the political divide. No one escaped his discerning eye or his stated philosophy: "Criticism where criticism is due."

When the *Beacon* ceased publication in 2005, Mr. Crutchfeld continued to publish his views via a website under the banner "Crusty's Corner." His many followers waited eagerly for his frequent postings.

Robert Quinn Crutchfeld always referred to himself as a 'newsboy,' harkening to the days when he delivered morning and evening newspaper editions to porches in Vallejo, CA, his hometown.

Today, Mother's Day, Gold Ridge mourns the loss of her beloved newsboy.

The article went on to list next of kin—spouse, children, grandchildren, siblings—and vague plans for a "celebration of life" to be held at some unspecified date. With the number of people expected to attend, the high school football stadium was suggested as the most likely venue.

That was the view from Sacramento. To the citizens of Gold Ridge, it was much more personal. Robert Crutchfeld was known to enjoy a shot of Old Bushmills chased with a pint of Guinness. In watering holes all around town, the toasts to Crusty Bob continued deep into the evening.

52

Lilly played the exchange with Dr. Patel over and over in her mind.

Did you know this man, Nurse Morgan?

Yes. Yes, I did. He was…he was family.

There was no doubt in her response, and yet it took a week for the *family* to claim Webb Johnson's body from the crowded morgue. Officers from the coroner's office, in full protective gear, searched his belongings at the Bitter Creek Hotel. They confirmed there were no living relatives.

Brett arranged for a local funeral home to retrieve Webb's body for cremation. The home delivered his ashes in a burnished pewter urn, leaving Brett and Ramona to ponder the next steps.

All of this occurred amid the drama surrounding Lilly and Don.

Lilly was ordered to self-quarantine for fourteen days to see if symptoms would develop from her exposure to COVID-19. She would be tested if symptoms developed, and if not, she'd be tested at the end of the fourteen-day period before being allowed to return to work. She spent the first day in isolation at Hotel Truro, but Ramona offered a better plan.

"Brett, what if we set up Lilly's apartment so that she can quarantine at home? That would give your dad a purpose, a mission, something to keep him so busy he won't have time to think about taking a drink. What do you think?"

"Hell of an idea. Let me talk to him. I think I can sell it."

It turned out to be an easy sale. Don, Brett, and Ramona went to work on Lilly's apartment, preparing for the balance of her quarantine. They cleaned and scrubbed and sanitized every square inch, then stood back to admire their work.

The apartment was a modern two-bedroom, two bath unit and the master bedroom had a private bath. Don would move into the second bedroom and use the guest bathroom. He would also become Lilly's caretaker, preparing meals to be left on a tray outside her door, delivering hot and cold beverages, managing laundry needs, and generally being on-call 24/7. He threw himself into the task with dogged determination.

✎

With Don taking care of Lilly, Brett and Ramona went to work on plans for Webster Johnson. They felt the need to do something to mark his passing. It would not be a community outpouring, such as the celebration of life planned for Robert Quinn Crutchfeld. But there had to be a way, however small, to say a proper goodbye.

They sat on the living room floor of their apartment, Ramona making notes on a yellow legal pad, brainstorming ideas. Crumpled balls of yellow paper began to accumulate as one idea after another bit the dust. Who could they count on to attend? Lilly was in quarantine with Don dedicated to her care, and when that was completed, Don was scheduled to enter rehab. Joey D had gone home to the Bay Area where a member of his family was stricken with the virus. The yellow balls multiplied. Brett took a break and went for five-mile run, followed by a cool shower.

Ramona knocked on the door as he toweled off. "Hey, babe. There's somebody here to see you."

"Yeah? Who is it?"

"Remember Webb's friend, Curley Grimble? He's waiting for you, outside on the steps. He didn't want to come in. He's out there wearing his mask, like a good citizen."

"Okay, tell him I'll be there in a minute."

Brett dressed quickly in jeans and a T-shirt. He donned a cloth mask, left the apartment, and found Curley sitting on the steps outside.

"Hey, Curley, good to see you. Sorry we have to meet out here." Brett sat on the upper step, a cautious ten feet from his guest.

"No problem, Brett. Hey…uh…I don't really know what to say. I'm so sorry about Webb. I know you two were close. I mean…" Curley's voice trailed off.

"Thanks, Curley. It means a lot that you came by. You knew him a long time, am I right?"

"Yeah, we crossed paths a couple of times in the minors. And we were roommates in Tacoma. They always had us black guys room together. We hung out a lot. Raised some serious hell, too." He laughed.

"You were roommates up in Tacoma?"

"Yeah, we were. He really had a great year in '64. I thought sure he'd be called up.

"He told us about that."

It was quiet for a moment. Curley continued. "Brett, there's something I wanted to talk to you about."

"Yeah?"

"See, I'm not with the Rockies anymore. They're letting scouts go, paring down the organization. I'm freelancing now, mostly representing college programs."

Brett wasn't sure what to say. "How's that working out?"

"Ah…what can I say. Times are tough. But look, Brett, have you thought about college, about transferring to a four-year school?"

"No, not much. Until all this happened, I was hoping to be drafted. Probably a lower round, but at least a chance to play pro ball…somewhere."

"You know they've cut the June draft from forty rounds down to five," Curley said. "Can you believe it? Five freakin' rounds! There's a whole lot of guys puttin' their dreams on hold right now. Instead of comin' out for the draft, they'll be staying in school another year. It's gonna cause a major logjam."

Brett mulled it over. He wasn't aware of the five-round decision, or its impacts.

"Anyway, I want you to know that I've had conversations with the head coach at CSU Chico. He is definitely interested, Brett. He really needs pitching, even with guys staying in school. He needs somebody who can step in and be a weekend starter."

"Yeah? I can do that."

"I know you can. You know baseball scholarships are partial, it wouldn't be a full ride, but it would cover tuition. And it's a damn good program. You'd attract some major league attention playing there."

"Geez, Curley. I don't know what to say."

"Give it some thought, Brett. It's a good program. And a good school. I know your old man was in tech. Any interest in Computer Science? They have a great curriculum there."

"No, not really my thing."

"How about education? You could be a teacher…and a coach… like Webb."

Brett would definitely think about it, because Curley Grimble was good at his job and knew how to plant seeds. This one found fertile ground. Brett had his Plan B, just as Ramona's father had suggested.

53

It was a short drive from the hotel near the Oakland airport to Bellena Isle Harbor in Alameda. Brett was at the wheel, Ramona beside him, Don and Lilly in the backseat of Don's BMW sedan. Lilly was fresh out of quarantine; no symptoms had developed, and she'd tested negative for coronavirus.

The four of them found this window, a two-day break, when all could be together to give Webb Johnson a proper sendoff. At Bellena Isle, they would connect with Joey DiFranco and Curley Grimble, and with a former client of Don's who kept his boat at the marina. Secure in the trunk of the BMW, wrapped in a beach towel, packed in a grocery bag, was the urn containing Webb's ashes.

They converged on the marina at 10:00 a.m. on Memorial Day 2020, everyone sporting a cloth face mask. Don bumped elbows with Al McMartin, his former client, CIO of an East Bay company. They exchanged the standard *How the hell are ya* greetings.

Al would be their skipper, piloting them across the bay in his Beneteau Swift Trawler 34, the spacious cabin more than large enough for the six passengers. He led them through the gate and onto the dock where his trawler was berthed. The script across the stern read, *Skip to Malou / Alameda, CA*.

"Y'all just make yourself at home. There's coffee, tea, water, and some bagels and cream cheese if you're hungry. It will take about 35 minutes to cross the bay. Should be a smooth ride, not much chop today."

Al went to the flying bridge while a boy who worked at the marina cast off the mooring lines. The boat pulled away from the dock and chugged out of the harbor, past the man-made breakwater. Al gradually pushed the throttle to full and cruised into the open waters of San Francisco Bay, the majestic Bay Bridge looming off the starboard bow. It was a clear and sunny day, the temperature expected to approach eighty degrees.

Brett and Ramona had planned a brief ceremony for the scattering of Webb's ashes. They would go around the cabin and ask each person to say a few words. The theme was simple: If you could speak to Webb, what would you say?

The *Skip to Malou* pulled into McCovey Cove and Al throttled back the engine. She drifted slowly, surrounded by the familiar landmarks—China Basin Park to the left, the Lefty O'Doul Bridge straight ahead, and the massive right field wall of Oracle Park to the right.

Brett felt his heart racing. It was time to begin. "Curley, would you like to lead off?"

"Sure. Well, Webb, all I have to say is you were a great teammate and roommate, and an even better friend. The time we shared was the best time of my life. And I promise that whatever happened in Tacoma, stays in Tacoma." He waited for the laughter to die down. "Godspeed, old friend."

Lilly was next. "Webb, you were a dear, sweet man who hit rock bottom and needed a lift. You rose up like a guardian angel, reaching out to help everyone around you. You were a wonderful addition to our family."

It was Don's turn. "Webb, I'm so happy I found you at Denny's back in December 2018. Where would we be without you? Where would *I* be? I saw you get sober and stay sober, and then do your best to help me. You are my inspiration, Webb. I'm gonna make it, and you'll be with me every day."

Everyone looked at Joey D and saw the tears in his eyes. "Webb, all I can say is thank you for bringing me along for the ride and making me believe in myself. I see a lot of seagulls and pigeons outside, but I'm hoping there will be a few mourning doves to keep you company."

Ramona glanced at Brett and began. "Webb, we grew to love you, simple as that. I'll never forget your kindness and your patience. I want you to know Brett and I are going to be married, and if we're blessed someday with a baby boy, his middle name will be Webster."

That left Brett with a giant lump in his throat. He took a moment to let it clear.

"Webb, you were an amazing coach, friend, mentor. I could never thank you enough for what you did for me. I think of all the times I was ready to quit, and you brought me back, again and again.

"We're gonna leave you here in McCovey Cove. I can look out and see the statue of Willie Mac with that beautiful swing of his. And around the corner by the main gate, there's the statue of Willie Mays. They're all here, Webb—Cepeda, Marichal, Perry. You're in good company. As they say, Forever Giant."

Brett and Ramona rose and stepped out of the cabin, onto the deck at the stern. Brett held Webb's urn in his hands. They looked down into the brackish green water of the bay, the prop of the trawler churning gently. Brett went out onto the fantail and removed the lid from the urn. He knelt on the platform, leaned close to the water, and spilled the ashes. A light breeze sent some ash trailing across the surface while most of the gritty matter sank into the cove.

Brett replaced the lid and turned to Ramona. "I think I'll keep this."

"Sure." She smiled at him.

He rotated the urn in his hands to read the inscription:

Webster Allan Johnson
August 9, 1940 – May 2, 2020

VELOCITY
LOCATION
MOVEMENT

54

Gold Ridge could not escape the turmoil that engulfed the nation. Hundreds crowded the square in front of City Hall to bear witness to the death of George Floyd. The town honored the words of John Donne:

> *Therefore, send not to know*
> *for whom the bell tolls,*
> *it tolls for thee.*

A podium and sound system were hastily installed so that the Mayor, the Chief of Police, and several faith leaders could call for justice, healing, and peace.

When the official speakers were through and the sound system unplugged, firebrands mounted the steps with bullhorns to lead the crowd in chants.

> *Black lives matter!*
> *Say his name! George Floyd!*
> *I can't breathe! I can't breathe!*

The several hundred gathered in the square provided unwitting cover for those bent on mayhem and destruction. Windows in the downtown business district were broken, the shops looted. Trash cans were set ablaze and anything that would burn went into the fire.

On the third night, the mayor declared a curfew to begin at sundown. As the sun set, the peaceful folk of Gold Ridge left the demonstration and headed home. The criminals did not. The small police force, aided by county sheriff's officers, stayed busy arresting looters and filling jail cells, while firefighters doused the flames.

It was a dichotomy, the righteous and the profane drawn by the same horrendous event—the murder of an unarmed black man in a city two thousand miles away.

⁓

Ramona and Brett made their way home, walking down Main Street away from City Hall, their cloth masks in place. They were joined by dozens of people leaving the demonstration, walking and talking quietly in the gathering dusk.

"I thought Chief Ramsdale gave a good speech tonight. Whataya think, babe?" Ramona looked up at Brett.

"Yeah..." He searched for words, then looked away.

"What? What is it, Brett?"

"You know when we chanted 'Black lives matter'? It made me think of Webb. He mattered."

"You got that right." Ramona smiled. "Anyway, I hope it's peaceful tonight. No crap like we had last night."

"Yeah. Let's hope."

The crowd paused at the intersection of First Street. Off to the east, several blocks away, something was on fire, flames leaping high into the air, black smoke billowing. Sirens screamed as the fire department rushed to the blaze.

Brett felt a knot in the pit of his stomach. He'd resigned himself to a summer without baseball. Now it looked like a summer without

peace. He would attend demonstrations tomorrow, and the next day, and the day after that—in Gold Ridge, Auburn, and Sacramento. He couldn't know then, standing at the corner of First and Main, that on the steps of the state capitol, he would grab the microphone and say, *I want to tell you about a man. His name was Webster Johnson, and I want you to know what he did for me, and my father, and our entire family. He died of COVID-19, and maybe, just maybe, he didn't have to. He was a Black man, and his life mattered....*

Brett reached for Ramona's hand and held it tight. He felt the sharp edge of the diamond ring on her finger, and it made him smile.

Dr. Bowman was right: One pitch at a time.

ACKNOWLEDGEMENTS

One Pitch at a Time enjoyed the benefit of several trusted first-readers, including Casey Dorman, Brian M. Biggs, Diana Carlson Pardee, and Tom Campbell. All these folks are writers and accomplished storytellers. Their feedback was invaluable, many times sending me into rewrite mode.

My friend Bruce Bigelow, who I've known since the Truman administration, read an early draft. Brucie, this is the new, improved edition. I hope you like it.

Diana Hwang took my concept for the cover and turned it into reality, just as she did with my novella, *Street Cred*. She is a joy to work with.

I close with a special thank you to Billie Kelpin, who, without knowing it, became my development editor. We began exchanging chapters of our works in progress, and I learned Billie has an amazing eye for detail and nuance. And she grew up in Milwaukee as a devoted fan of the Braves and a "really cute" Hall of Fame third baseman named Eddie Mathews. Perfect qualifications for a baseball-themed story! Billie, I can't thank you enough.

Printed in the United States
by Baker & Taylor Publisher Services